"It's No Wonder People Fall In Love In The Desert."

Prince Omar's jaw tightened at Jana's words, but she was looking at the distant dunes and did not notice. "Do you think so?"

The tone of the sheikh's voice startled her, so full of cynical unhappiness that she turned and blinked at him. "Don't you?"

"I have never loved the desert or thought it inspired love," he said flatly.

She watched him for a moment under the starlight. "What do you love, then?"

He gave a bark of laughter. "You speak as if everyone must love something."

"A person would have to be very hard not to love someone, some part of the world," Jana said mildly. "So hard they couldn't be called human."

"Oh, I am human," he replied, reaching through the moonlight to touch her hair. "And I have you to remind me that I am a man...."

Dear Reader,

This May we invite you to delve into six delicious new titles from Silhouette Desire!

We begin with the brand-new title you've been eagerly awaiting from the incomparable Ann Major. *Love Me True,* our May MAN OF THE MONTH, is a riveting reunion romance offering the high drama and glamour that are Ann's hallmarks.

The enjoyment continues in FORTUNE'S CHILDREN: THE BRIDES with *The Groom's Revenge* by Susan Crosby. A young working woman is swept off her feet by a wealthy CEO who's married her with more than love on his mind—he wants revenge on the father who never claimed her, Stuart Fortune. A "must read" for all you fans of Daphne Du Maurier's *Rebecca!*

Barbara McMahon's moving story *The Cowboy and the Virgin* portrays the awakening—both sensual and emotional—of an innocent young woman who falls for a ranching Romeo. But can she turn the tables and corral *him?* Beverly Barton's emotional miniseries 3 BABIES FOR 3 BROTHERS concludes with *Having His Baby*. Experience the birth of a father as well as a child when a rugged rancher is transformed by the discovery of his secret baby—and the influence of her pretty mom. Then, in her exotic SONS OF THE DESERT title, *The Solitary Sheikh,* Alexandra Sellers depicts a hard-hearted sheikh who finds happiness with his daughters' aristocratic tutor. And *The Billionaire's Secret Baby* by Carol Devine is a compelling marriage-of-convenience story.

Now more than ever, Silhouette Desire offers you the most passionate, powerful and provocative of sensual romances. Make yourself merry this May with all six Desire novels—and buy another set for your mom or a close friend for Mother's Day!

Enjoy!

Joan Marlow Golan
Senior Editor, Silhouette Desire

Please address questions and book requests to:
Silhouette Reader Service
U.S.: 3010 Walden Ave., P.O. Box 1325, Buffalo, NY 14269
Canadian: P.O. Box 609, Fort Erie, Ont. L2A 5X3

THE SOLITARY
SHEIKH
ALEXANDRA SELLERS

SILHOUETTE *Desire*®
Published by Silhouette Books
America's Publisher of Contemporary Romance

for my sister, Margaret,
who helped

SILHOUETTE BOOKS

ISBN 0-373-76217-8

THE SOLITARY SHEIKH

Look us up on-line at: http://www.romance.net

Printed in U.S.A.

Books by Alexandra Sellers

Silhouette Desire

Sheikh's Ransom #1210
The Solitary Sheikh #1217

Silhouette Intimate Moments

The Real Man #73
The Male Chauvinist #110
The Old Flame #154
The Best of Friends #348
The Man Next Door #406
A Gentleman and a Scholar #539
The Vagabond #579
Dearest Enemy #635
Roughneck #689
Bride of the Sheikh #771
Wife on Demand #833

*Sons of the Desert

Silhouette Yours Truly

A Nice Girl Like You
Not Without a Wife!
Shotgun Wedding
Occupation: Millionaire

ALEXANDRA SELLERS

was born in Ontario, and raised in Ontario and Saskatchewan. She first came to London to attend the Royal Academy of Dramatic Art and fell in love with the city. Later she returned to make it her permanent home. Now married to an Englishman, she lives near Hampstead Heath. As well as writing romance, she teaches a course called "How To Write a Romance Novel" in London several times a year.

Because of a much-regretted allergy she can have no resident cat, but she receives regular charitable visits from three cats who are neighbors.

Readers can write to her at P.O. Box 9449, London, NW3 2WH, England.

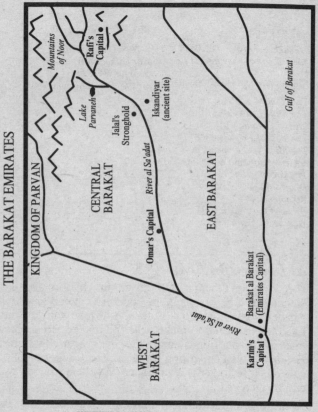

THE BARAKAT EMIRATES

- Mountains of Noor
- Rafi's Capital
- KINGDOM OF PARVAN
- Lake Parvaneh
- Jalal's Stronghold
- Iskandiyar (ancient site)
- CENTRAL BARAKAT
- River al Sa'adat
- EAST BARAKAT
- Gulf of Barakat
- Omar's Capital
- Barakat al Barakat (Emirates Capital)
- WEST BARAKAT
- River al Sa'adat
- Karim's Capital

SHEIKH'S RANSOM, *Prince Karim's story*, April 1999
THE SOLITARY SHEIKH, *Prince Omar's story*, May 1999
BELOVED SHEIKH, *Prince Rafi's story*, June 1999

Available only from Silhouette Desire.

Omar's Inheritance
The Cup of Happiness

To Prince Omar's lot fell the Kingdom of Central Barakat, a land of sometimes rich, sometimes desolate desert, and the high, rugged, white-capped mountains of Noor with their many valleys. To him also was given the cup of his ancient ancestor Jalal, a magnificent pedestal cup of ruby, emerald and gold that was said to confer happiness on its owner. It had not conferred happiness on Omar. From the moment his father's will had granted him the cup, his life had seemed a bitter betrayal.

There was once a king of ancient and noble lineage who ruled over a land that had been blessed by God. This land,

Barakat, lying on the route of one of the old Silk Roads, had for centuries received the cultural influences of many different worlds. Its geography, too, was diverse: it bordered the sea; then the desert, sometimes bleak with its ancient ruins, sometimes golden and studded with oases, stretched inland for many miles, before meeting the foothills of snow-capped mountains that captured the rain clouds and forced them to deliver their burden in the rich valleys. It was a land of magic and plenty and a rich and diverse heritage.

But it was also a land of tribal rivalries and not infrequent skirmishes. Because the king had the ancient blood of the Quraishi kings in his veins, no one challenged his right to the throne, but many of the tribal chieftains whom he ruled were in constant jealousy over their lands and rights against the others.

One day, the king of this land fell in love with a foreign woman. Promising her that he would never take another wife, he married her and made her his queen. This beloved wife gave him two handsome sons. The king loved them as his own right hand. Crown Prince Zaid and his brother were all that he could wish for in his sons—handsome, noble, brave warriors, and popular with his people. As they attained the age of majority, the sheikh could look forward to his own death without fear for his country, for if anything should happen to the Crown Prince, his brother Aziz would step into his shoes and be equally popular with the people and equally strong among the tribes.

Then one day, tragedy struck the sheikh and his wife. Both their sons were killed in the same accident. Now his own death became the great enemy to the old man, for with it, he knew, would come certain civil war as the tribal chieftains vied for supremacy.

His beloved wife understood all his fears, but she was by now too old to hope to give him another heir. One day, when all the rituals of mourning were complete, the queen

*said to her husband, "According to the law, you are enti-
tled to four wives. Take, therefore, my husband, three new
wives, that God may bless one of them with a son to inherit
your throne."*

*The sheikh thanked her for releasing him from his prom-
ise. A few weeks later, on the same day so that none should
afterwards claim supremacy, the sheikh married three
beautiful young women, and that night, virile even in his
old age, he visited each wife in turn, no one save himself
knowing in which order he visited them. To each wife he
promised that if she gave him a son, her son would inherit
the throne of Barakat.*

*The sheikh was more virile than he knew. Each of his
new wives conceived, and gave birth, nine months later, to
a lusty son. And each was jealous for her own son's inheritance. From that moment the sheikh's life became a
burden to him, for each of his new young wives had different reasons for believing that her own son should be
named the rightful heir to the throne.*

*The Princess Goldar, whose exotically hooded green eyes
she had bequeathed to her son, Omar, based her claim on
the fact that she herself was a descendant of the ancient
royal family of her own homeland, Parvan.*

*The Princess Nargis, mother of Rafi and descended from
the old Mughal emperors of India, had in addition given
birth two days before the other two wives, thus making her
son the firstborn.*

*The Princess Noor, mother of Karim, claimed the inher-
itance for her son by right of blood—she alone of the wives
was an Arab of noble descent, like the sheikh himself. Who
but her son to rule the desert tribesmen?*

*The sheikh hoped that his sons would solve his dilemma
for him, that one would prove more princely than the others. But as they grew to manhood, he saw that each of them
was, in his own way, worthy of the throne, that each had*

*the nobility the people would look for in their king, and
talents that would benefit the kingdom were he to rule.*

*When his sons were eighteen years old, the sheikh knew
that he was facing death. As he lay dying, he saw each of
his young wives in turn. To each of them again he promised
that her son would inherit. Then he saw his three sons
together, and on them he laid his last command. Then, last
of all, he saw the wife and companion of his life, with whom
he had seen such happiness and such sorrow. To her willing care he committed his young wives and their sons, with
the assistance of his vizier, Nizam al Mulk, whom he appointed Regent jointly with her.*

*When he died the old sheikh's will was revealed: the
kingdom was to be divided into three principalities. Each
of his sons inherited one principality and its palace. In
addition, they each inherited one of the ancient Signs of
Kingship.*

*It was the will of their father that they should consult the
Grand Vizier Nizam al Mulk for as long as he lived, and
appoint another mutual Grand Vizier upon his death, so
that none would have partisan advice in the last resort.*

*Their father's last command had been this: that his sons
should never take up arms against each other or any of
their descendants, and that his sons and their descendants
should always come to each other's aid in times of trouble.
The sheikh's dying curse would be upon the head of any
who violated this command, and upon his descendants for
seven generations.*

*So the three princes grew to maturity under the eye of
the old queen and the vizier, who did their best to prepare
the princes for the future. When they reached the age of
twenty-five, they came into their inheritance. Then each
prince took his own Sign of Kingship and departed to his
own palace and his own kingdom, where they lived in peace
and accord with one another, as their father had commanded.*

One

A black stallion, its tail tossing, galloped over the desert. Its hooves thundered against the hard sand, sending notice of its presence for miles on the silent air. His sweat-glossed sable coat glistened, and gold threads in the embroidered saddlecloth and gold studs in the black bridle were picked out by the rays of the early-morning sun just rising over the rugged white mountains in the distance.

The tall, straight figure of the rider on its back seemed one with the graceful horse as the beast pounded towards a rushing, roaring river. The man's hair, as black as the stallion's pelt, waved thickly back from a high forehead, stirred by the wind of their speed. His slim, broad-shouldered body moved in rhythm with the horse as his knees urged it faster and faster, until it seemed that the rider intended to jump the river that now cut across the horse's path.

The feat would be impossible over the broad, wild torrent. Yet the man urged the horse on towards the wild rush of water, and the horse obeyed. At the last moment, just when it seemed as if its only choice was to dash itself and its rider into the churning waters, he pulled up. The horse reared and snorted; his forelegs danced on air and came to rest a few inches from the edge.

On closer view, it could be seen that both the man's hair and the horse's mane were not completely black, but were threaded with strands of silver. The man's broad, intelligent forehead was pulled into a frown over deep green, troubled eyes.

They paused there, horse and rider, while the man scanned the horizon and the horse stamped and snorted nervously at the noisy river. The frowning eyes seemed to take no pleasure from the sight of the rugged expanse of desert turned golden by the rising sun, nor the vigorous blue-black of the chilly river that rushed by at his horse's feet, nor the ferocious white-topped mountains in the distance. His small pointed beard and moustache neatly framed a once-generous mouth that now seemed twisted with sorrow and bitterness. His eyes gazed across the river down towards the ocean, which he knew was there, in the distance, invisible, indistinguishable from the sky.

His brother's land. The river marked the boundary of the land his father had bequeathed to him. Everything he saw on the other side, including the miles of distant shoreline, belonged to one of his brothers. If he turned to ride west he would, after many miles, come to the border he shared with his second brother.

His brothers. He had no brothers now. His father and mother were dead, his wife was dead, his brothers were lost to him. What did he have left in the world? A land of desert and mountain, much of it inhospitable, and even so, his right to rule over it was disputed by a fool who would stop at nothing to gain power. Two young daughters, whom he scarcely knew and could not love.

He did not love anyone, he realized with the curious enlightenment that recognition of the obvious sometimes brings. He had loved his father, but his father was dead, and had betrayed him in death, leaving him this inhospitable land. If he had ever loved his mother, she had killed that love by her ignorant ambition for him. She had wanted him to be king, without ever thinking of his happiness, and she had destroyed all chance of happiness for him when she had forced him to marry a woman he had found it impossible to love. And her ambitions had backfired when, long after his father had died, leaving him the least share of the kingdom, his wife had borne only daughters.

He had once loved his brothers, but they had betrayed him and their father's last command. His wife had died as a result, and though he had not loved her as a woman, as the passionate partner of his destiny he had once, long ago, dreamed of meeting, he had felt responsible for her and suffered at the loss.

His heart was cold and hard, as toughened as his body. Except for the basic sexual needs which there were many women willing to satisfy, he had no desires now, no love—only a diamond determination to keep this land, inhospitable as it was, under his own hand, and if possible pass it on to his daughters. He had no desire, even, to love. He wanted nothing that would disturb his hard reserve, his ability to face, without protest, whatever the world handed him.

He had no son. His daughters might be rejected by the tribes, they might never be allowed to inherit. In that case his land would be divided by the heirs of his brothers, and his name would disappear from the earth; but he wanted no wife, and he would not take another for the sake of producing a more acceptable heir. He wanted nothing from life now.

Minutes passed. The sun rose a little further in the sky to his left, disentangling itself from the mountaintops so that their shadow retreated across the foothills, revealing the huddle of houses in the village that had been his resting place in the night. Still the man made no signal to the restive beast.

It was the sound of hooves that roused him at last from his reverie. The faintest signal from the man's knees turned the horse in the direction of the noise, and then he cursed himself for a fool. They had crept up on him, and now they were spread out in a line between him and the safety of the foothills. Six riders, their white burnouses blowing in the wind as they rode at him, their rifles held in one hand above their heads, their throats giving forth the high ululation of attack.

The horse tossed its head, almost making the man drop the rifle that he swiftly withdrew from its home on the saddle. Urging the horse into a gallop towards them, guiding only with his knees, the reins loose on its neck, the man fired the rifle three times in quick succession without raising it to his shoulder, and three men as quickly cried out. Two rifles and one man fell into the sand, but still three horses came on towards him.

They did not want to kill him—he had that advantage. They wanted him captive, whereas he did not care whether any of them lived or died. If he killed them, they would lie in the desert until their fellow tribesmen came and collected the bodies. If they escaped, hurt or unhurt, they would return to their desert home and their leader. He wanted no rebel captives in his prisons, providing a rallying cause for the disenchanted.

He fired again as they were almost on top of him, and a horse stumbled into another and two riders were brought down. He galloped past the last rider and quickly urged the black stallion to wheel till he faced his attackers again.

There was one man still on his horse.

"We meet again, son of Daud!" called the bandit, and now the man recognized the rider in the centre of the splintered group.

"For the last time," Prince Hajji Omar Durran ibn Daud

ibn Hassan al Quraishi agreed grimly. He raised his rifle, but his attacker flung down his own gun into the dust. "My gun is useless!" the bandit leader cried.

For a moment two men on two heaving, sweating horses faced each other with the desert dust swirling between them. Through the sights and the dust Omar saw the man who wanted his throne, whose attempts to gain it had caused the death of his wife. His finger tightened on the trigger.

"You are a warrior, not an executioner, Prince of the People!"

Not disturbing the aim of his rifle, Prince Omar lifted his head and gazed at the man. The two were close enough to see each other's eyes.

At last Omar lowered his rifle. "Jalal, son of the bandit, be warned!" he called. "At our next meeting you will be dependent on the mercy of God. I will show none!" Then he wheeled his mount and with urgent knees encouraged it to a gallop again. Once he turned in the saddle to look back at his attackers. None showed any intention of following or firing at him. Beneath him the exhausted horse galloped on.

"Darling, take the Rolls," her mother pleaded, in her lead-crystal voice. "It's going to be a very hot day, and anyway, parking will be impossible. Let Michael drive you."

"Michael will get just as hot as I would," Jana said. "Why should he take the heat for me?"

"Because Michael is a chauffeur." Her mother ignored the joke with the irritated calm of one having to explain the same thing for the millionth time but determined not to let it bother her. "It's his job."

Well, it was and it wasn't. For the first seven years of her life, until her parents had separated, chauffeured limousines had been a normal part of Jana's existence. But then she had moved to Calgary, where her mother had taken a job. There, apart from going to a private school, Jana had led a pretty ordinary life. When her parents reconciled after ten years—

an event Jana had longed for every day of those years—she had found that the return to her old life in the Scottish manor house that was her father's ancestral home was more difficult than she had imagined. She was impatient of the restrictions that both her parents suddenly seemed to want to impose on her, in keeping with her position as the daughter of a viscount descended from the Royal Stewarts.

After university, determined to make some contribution to the world that was a little more intensive than opening the next charity ball or fete, Jana had gone to teach school in an underprivileged area of London. Her parents had not objected too strongly until they discovered that instead of living in their apartment in posh Belgravia, where they kept a housekeeper and chauffeur full-time, she was determined to rent a place not far from her school and drive her own little Mini. But as time passed and no disaster befell her, they had stopped protesting.

Last week the school year had ended, and with it, the teaching career Jana had once looked forward to with such excitement, but which had been an indescribable mixture of joys and sorrows, frustrations and achievement. The sorrows and frustrations had won in the end.

Her mother was in town now to discuss Jana's future. She had been horrified to discover that that future was already all but decided, and in what manner—Jana was preparing for a final interview for a job to go abroad and teach English to a foreign family.

"In any case, he won't, because the Rolls is air-conditioned."

Jana sighed. "Why is it such a big deal, Mother?"

"If you will insist on taking a job with some oriental despot he should know who you are."

"He knows who I am. I've never been so thoroughly vetted in my life. I think he's checked the family all the way back to Robert the Bruce," Jana pointed out mildly, looking at her mother curiously. "Why do you say he's a despot? I've been told it's a wealthy family with mining interests."

"Darling, all important families in the Middle East are connected to the ruling house in any country. It's simply the way things are."

Jana forbore to suggest that things were not so different right here in England. "No one has said a word about royal connections."

Her mother shrugged. "Even so, it beats me why you imagine you'll meet less restriction there, Jana. In half those countries the women are being forced to wear the veil again."

"I've been assured that the family and the country are liberal on the issue of women's rights. And after all, the job is teaching English to the seven- and nine-year-old *daughters* of the house, so they can't be that backward. And anything will be less restricting than not being allowed to teach with a method that works," Jana added, with a dark thread of bitterness in her voice.

Her mother frowned worriedly. "You are so impulsive," she observed for the thousandth time in Jana's life. "Darling, please think it over. Please don't go."

"I want to get away, Mother." She repeated it doggedly, like a mantra, because she had nothing else to say.

The pain was still raw.

"You are not absolutely prohibited from using these teaching methods, Miss Stewart," the inquiry board had announced, and she had known then that what was coming was the end of her career in teaching, "but you may not abandon the national curriculum. You must teach first and foremost by the established method but may use your own methods as a supplement if you wish."

"It isn't *possible* to teach both!" Jana had shouted. She had pointed out a hundred times that her method worked, that it actually *taught children to read*. In addition, because the children were achieving something, there was far less class disruption.

The national curriculum method for teaching reading bored and defeated them, and they became unmanageable. When she had taught it, she, like so many others in the system, had been reduced to acting as a cross between a babysitter and prison guard.

The council had sat impassive while she railed at them for their narrow-minded ignorance and cowardly sticking to ineffective methods, but when she resigned they had accepted it with obvious relief. She had finished out the school year, but as of a week ago, Jana was unemployed.

Of course, the media had been on her side. It was just the kind of story they loved, but Jana had very soon tired of being fodder for the entertainment industry that masqueraded as news broadcasting, and in any case her story had a brief lifespan. It would take more than newspaper articles and talk shows to change the national curriculum, though a generation of children had already emerged from the schools unable to read.

Fighting was what was needed, but Jana had temporarily run out of the famous Stewart fighting energy. She felt like her distant ancestor, Bonnie Prince Charlie, after the Battle of Culloden: defeated. Her father urged her to enter politics and run for parliament—that, too, was a part of the family heritage—and one day she might do that. But for the moment, Jana just wanted to get away and lick her wounds.

The ad for a private English tutor to "an important family in the small but prosperous Barakat Emirates" had caught her eye two months ago. The position was for a minimum of one year. She knew it was the escape she needed.

"There are better ways to get away than a job in the Barakat Emirates," her mother said.

Jana shrugged. Her mother's suggestion of a sailing holiday in the Maldives or a villa in Greece, either of which friends could be counted on to supply at short notice, *had* tempted her…until she saw what her mother was really planning. Jana had no intention of taking such a holiday if Peter was also going to be a guest—and her mother would make certain that Peter was a guest. Peter was the man her whole family adored.

"Mother, we've been over it."

"I really think, Jana, that a few weeks in—"

"Mother."

"Yes, darling."

"I am not going to marry Peter," Jana said, slowly and unmistakably.

"Oh, darling, why do you keep saying that? He's so right—"

Jana couldn't help laughing. Her mother was completely transparent. Peter was right for her parents, and would be a great brother for Julian and Jessica, her younger sister and brother. She knew all that. Unfortunately, he was not right for Jana. They agreed about nothing in life. She sighed and shrugged. She was so tired of fighting. *Please, God, let me get this job,* she prayed silently. *Don't let me end up married to Peter.*

Her laughter cut her mother off. She looked at Jana and lifted her hands resignedly. "At least take the Rolls," she urged.

Jana gave in. She knew her mother had manipulated her, had made it seem like a small concession when she was holding out on a major issue, and her own weakness frightened her. Her resistance was low. If the whole family started pressing her to marry Peter…Jana clenched her jaw. If she was offered the job she would take it even if the advertiser *was* an oriental despot.

Two

An hour later Jana slipped gracefully out of the back seat
of the navy Rolls and into the heat of the city streets, looking as fresh as a spring morning. She stood for a moment
looking up at the facade of the Dorchester Hotel. Under the
caress of the hot summer sun it had a rich, satisfied glow.

"Thank you, Michael," she murmured to the chauffeur.

"Good luck, Miss," he said. "I hope you get the job."

"Thank you. I do, too," she said, a little grimly.

She thought her chances were good. Her experience was
right for the job. She had had three interviews over the past
six weeks—all with intermediaries—and she knew the
numbers had been whittled down to a shortlist of three or
four. Now the father of the children she would teach was
in town and she was meeting him for the first time. She
had been told that their mother was dead.

She flashed a quick smile at the doorman as he held the
door for her, and he seemed to take in her slim, vibrant

figure, her glowing red hair, wide-spaced eyes and dramatic flair with one comprehensive, appreciative glance that managed to indicate that he wouldn't mind holding the door all day for her.

"Good afternoon, Miss. Lovely day," he offered.

Then she was being ushered to the enquiry desk, where a stern, handsome, dark-eyed Barakati took her in tow, led her into an elevator, and then, as the doors closed, said, "Forgive me, but may I have your handbag?"

Jana stiffened. "What?"

"I request to search your handbag, Miss Stewart."

She stared at him down her nose. "Certainly not!" she said, in her best imitation of her mother.

The minion shrugged. "I am sorry, Madame, I must insist."

"Nothing was said to me at any time about being searched!"

The elevator arrived at the floor and stopped, but he had turned a key in the panel and the doors did not open.

"*I* say it, Madame."

"And who are you?"

"I am Ashraf Durran, cousin and Cup Companion to Omar Durran ibn Daud ibn Hassan al Quraishi," he said, with a nod of such regal condescension that she blinked. "Please, Miss Stewart, allow me to search you. He is waiting for you."

Jana hadn't run away from the restrictions of her own family life all these years to go to work now for someone who had their staff physically searched and who was apparently worried about assassination attempts. Maybe her mother was right.

She asked with angry amusement, "Whose pay, exactly, does he imagine I'm in?"

"There are many fools in the world, Miss Stewart," the man said simply. "Please," he said, lifting his hands in a gesture inviting reason.

Her hands tightened on her bag. She was damned if she'd submit to this! "I was invited here for an interview, and no one said anything about being searched. I think there's been a mistake," she said firmly.

Ashraf Durran stared at her, shrugged and reached into his pocket. For a chilling moment she thought the narrow black object he pulled out was a gun. She laughed with reflexive relief when he started to speak into it. After a moment he said, *"Baleh, baleh,"* and put it back in his pocket.

"I must search you and your bag, Madame," he said.

"Or?"

"Or escort you back downstairs."

She glared furiously at him. "Well, *do* tha—" she began, but immediately broke off. She thought of Peter, of the vacation her mother would engineer—for Jana *and* Peter—if she did not get this job.

She handed her bag to Ashraf Durran, waited as he searched it and handed it back to her. "Excuse me," he said, and she gasped as he reached for her and then stood in cold, stony fury as he ran his hands lightly, impersonally over her body.

"Thank you," he said. "I am sorry for the necessity." Then he turned the key and the elevator doors opened.

She stepped out into a large furnished foyer. A massive mirror directly opposite reflected her image. She was relieved to see that her irritation did not show. In her white dress she was neat and cool looking. There were several men, all in Western suits, but some wearing burnouses in addition, standing and sitting around the room, and they all turned to watch her progress as Ashraf Durran led her across to a door. She had the humiliating conviction that they all knew that she had just been searched.

Ashraf Durran tapped on the door and opened it. As the door opened into the elegantly furnished hotel sitting room, the two occupants turned towards her and got to their feet.

Behind them an expanse of Hyde Park showed green through a wide window. One man, she saw, was the old man with grey hair, tall, thin, and perfectly erect, whom she had met at a previous interview. Hadi al Hatim's dark eyes sparkled with a smile of welcome.

The other was much younger—in his mid-to-late thirties, she thought—a little taller, lean, a good build. He had sea green eyes, strong cheekbones, a broad forehead, thick black hair and a neat devil's beard. His expression was hard and closed. He might as well have been carved from stone, for all the feeling she got from him. He did not smile.

"Miss Jana Stewart, Your Highness," Hadi al Hatim presented her, then put out his hand. Jana shivered as she put out her own hand to take it. "Miss Stewart, it is a pleasure to meet you again. This is His Serene Highness Sheikh Omar ibn Daud, the Prince of Central Barakat."

"*Prince?*" she repeated on a wailing note. "My mother was right! Oh, *damn* it!"

Of course she shouldn't have said it. His Serene Highness Prince Omar ibn Daud stiffened—Jana didn't think it was possible to get any stiffer than he already was, but he managed it—and stared at her from eyes as cold as the green, green sea.

"What is the matter, Miss Stewart?" He spoke with an accent, in a deep, hard, unresponsive voice.

"You were described to me as an influential Barakati family with mining interests!" she said.

There was an arrogant tilt to his head. "We own the gold and the emerald mines of the mountains of Noor."

"Congratulations!" she said dryly. She was irritated by his icily arrogant manner. She realized that she had no idea how to greet a sheikh. Should she curtsey? She was pretty sure that the curtsey was a purely Western tradition, but the Eastern genuflection before princes, if her memory served, was the kind of prostration where you touched your nose to the ground, and that seemed too incongruous, even for the Dorchester.

"But I don't want to work in a palace. And I do think I might have—"

Been warned, she was going to say, but he cut across her. "Why not?" His voice was flat, emotionless. Not even curiosity showed.

The interruption annoyed her, and she snapped, "Partly for all the reasons that make you think you can interrupt me whenever you like."

He stared at her. "Miss Stewart, I do not understand your hostility. You seemed to my vizier very eager to take this job." He glanced at Hadi al Hatim, but the old man, the suspicion of a smile at one corner of his mouth, was saying nothing. "What is the reason for your attitude?"

"I've just been *body searched* in the damned elevator," Jana said, waving an indignant arm back towards the door. "There's an army of bodyguards out there, and it turns out to be because you're a prince, that's the reason!"

"I have no army of bodyguards," he informed her flatly. "You are not yet a member of my household staff. When you are, you will not be searched when you approach me."

Approach me. He sounded like something out of the fifteenth century. "That's not the point. The point is, I wasn't told I was applying for a job in a royal family."

"Now you have been told. You do not want the job?"

Faced with the stark decision, Jana suddenly, belatedly, began to think. To wonder if she was handling this in the best way. Not for nothing did her family and friends accuse her of impulsiveness.

One thing was sure—her mother and Peter would be quick to take advantage of her situation if she agreed with what His Serene Highness had just said and walked out of here.

"Well—I..." She hesitated and bit her lip.

The vizier intervened. "Miss Stewart, before this meeting, His Highness and I had decided that you were very much the best candidate for the job. If you are now determined not to take the job, there is nothing to be said. If you are in doubt, I suggest you sit down and discuss the matter.''

It was a very gracious way out.

"All right," she said gratefully.

Prince Omar indicated the sofa and they sat down, the prince in a chair set at an angle to her. Hadi al Hatim retired to a window embrasure.

"In your last interview, I think, you were informed that the job requires that you will live with us, teaching two girls," he said. "You are aware of their ages and their level of proficiency." Although his use of English seemed very good, she sensed that he did not really feel comfortable with the language, and she wondered why.

"The only thing I wasn't told about them, I think, was that they are princesses." Jana looked into his eyes, and was locked by a gaze that seemed to both draw and repel her at the same time. She felt the surge of a mixture of feelings—surprise, confusion, discomfort, nervousness, irritation. "I'm right in that? They are your daughters?"

"Yes, they are," he said, without any hint of parental feeling. Just stating a cold, hard fact. Jana wondered if there were someone with a little more warmth of feeling closer to the girls. "If you have questions, you may ask them now."

"How much would you personally expect to dictate terms in my teaching?"

"Terms?" he repeated, frowning slightly. "We do not have school terms. The princesses are taught entirely by tutors within the palace. Most of them are now absent for the summer. I prefer that you start now because the princesses have been without English lessons for some months."

She laughed lightly at the misunderstanding. "No, no, I

meant..." She flailed for another way of explaining, and then gasped as his face hardened and his eyes glinted with cold rage.

"My English is very far from perfect, Miss Stewart. I hope you will not be moved to laugh at every error I will make."

Jana sat up straight. "I was *not* laughing at any error!" she said indignantly.

Prince Omar raised a disbelieving eyebrow. "No? What caused your amusement?"

She gritted her teeth. "The mutual misunderstanding!"

"I see."

"Do you forbid laughter in the palace?"

He sat for a moment watching her. She didn't think she had ever seen such resignation in a human face.

"No, I do not forbid it," he answered, but she could see that laughter rarely happened, even if it was not actively forbidden. She was starting to feel seriously sorry for his daughters, raised with such a curb as this cold-hearted father must place on their spirits.

"What are your daughters' names?" she asked involuntarily.

His dark green gaze flicked briefly towards Hadi al Hatim and then back to her. "Masha and Kamala are their usual names."

"*Kaw*-meh-leh," she repeated carefully. "Masha. They're both very pretty names." She smiled. "Masha. Isn't that Russian?"

"Masha is short for Mashouka, which means *beloved* in Parvani, my mother's tongue. It is true that I spent many years in Russia. There it is short for Maria. But I did not intentionally give my daughter a Russian name."

He sounded as though it would be the last thing he'd do. "If you hated it so much, why were you there?" she asked impulsively. Speaking without thinking was one of Jana's

most determined faults. By the time she reminded herself
to think before she spoke, Jana had usually already spoken.

"I did not say I hated it." Another glance at the silent
vizier. "I attended univ—"

"But you did hate it."

His eyelids drooped, as if to hide his reaction from her,
and, released from his gaze, she suddenly was free to notice
how physically attractive he was. His face and head were
beautifully shaped, and both the curving eyelids and the
full lower lip held a sensual promise. His beard gave him
the look of a Hollywood pirate. But the coldness in his
eyes seemed to undo all that.

He heaved an impatient sigh.

"Yes, I did hate it. Why do you insist on this, Miss
Stewart? Is it important to you?"

Jana's cheeks were suddenly warm. "I'm sorry," she
said.

He was watching her curiously. "Do you yourself have
some connection with Russia?"

"None at all," she replied hastily, hoping he would not
press the point. She could hardly confess that she had felt
an impulse to make him admit to some feeling! So the
Prince of Central Barakat was withdrawn! It was not her
business.

"Do you have a picture of them?" she asked.

"Of the princesses?" He frowned, as though the request
was unusual. "I don't know—" He turned in his chair and
called to his vizier, "Do we have such a photograph,
Khwaja?"

Hadi al Hatim smiled and crossed to the table in front
of the sofa where they were sitting. He pulled a file out of
a briefcase and extracted a colour ten-by-eight photograph,
handing it to the prince. At that moment the Cup Companion who had searched her appeared at the door, and the
vizier crossed the room and went out with him, closing the
door behind him.

"Baleh," Omar replied to something the vizier said as he left. He hardly glanced at the photo before passing it to Jana.

With a little shiver of response at his clinical coldness in looking at a photograph of his daughters, Jana leaned forward to take the picture. In one of those slightly awkward moments of misjudgement, both she and Prince Omar moved a few inches more than either expected the other to do, and their hands brushed. She drew in her breath with a little shock.

Two young girls half smiled at the camera, their arms around each other. They were very pretty, and would probably be beautiful when they got older. Wide dark eyes, delicately shaped eyebrows, their father's curving eyelids and full mouth. Beautiful, but lacking confidence, their gaze at the camera shy, their smiles tentative. Jana found herself feeling as protective towards them as she had for any of her schoolchildren from troubled homes. Wealth and position had never protected children against misery, she reminded herself, and these two had lost their mother, and, if His Serene Highness's attitude was anything to go by, had never had a real father.

And yet, one was called Beloved. She wondered who had chosen that name.

"They are very lovely. You must be proud of them."

"They are like their mother. She was considered a great beauty," he said, as if he were discussing a database or import duty.

"What does Kamala mean?" she asked, looking up from the photograph to discover that he was watching her.

"It means *perfect,* Miss Stewart." He paused, and they looked at each other. In the silence, they were abruptly aware that they were alone together in the room. Prince Omar lifted a long slender hand to his dark beard and stroked it, and she watched the motion of his fingers without being aware that she did so.

She could not think of anything to say. There were words, but they seemed caught in her throat. She stared at his mouth, full but held so firmly in check. His lips moved, and she caught her breath on a silent gasp.

"Your own name has a meaning in our language," he said. "Jana."

He lengthened the first *a. Jahn-eh.*

Jana swallowed. "What does it mean?"

"Soul," he said. "Really, 'the soul of'—it is incomplete. *Jan-am* means *my soul,* for example. What is your middle name?"

Jana shivered. His deep voice had softened on the words, and he was watching her as he said them, and her skin responded as if to a touch.

"Roxane."

"This also is a Parvani word. *Roshan* means 'light.' Therefore your names together mean 'light's soul,' or 'a soul of light.'"

Jana swallowed and nodded. "I see," she said. "Thank you."

There was a pause while the prince considered the sheaf of papers in his hand. She recognized her résumé and application, but the rest was written in the Arabic alphabet.

"You are descended from the royal family of Scotland."

"We lost that battle many generations ago, Your Highness."

"But you will have an understanding of royal life that the others did not have. This is always the problem, that the foreign teachers cannot understand the restrictions. You, I think, would understand."

She thought, *Oh, yes, I would understand. It's just what I've always fought against, the restrictions.* She looked down at the photo of those two questioning, uncertain little faces, and a well of pity washed up in her.

"Yes," she said.

"And your work in the poorest schools tells me that you

understand the nature of duty. The princesses must also understand their duty.''

Poor, poor little princesses. She looked again at the photo still in her hand. He was going to offer her the job. And in spite of everything, she realized, she still wanted it. Not entirely for the sake of the little lost-looking princesses. But for her own sake, too. However cold the sheikh was, however restricted the environment, it would only be for a year. If she ended up married to Peter…that sentence would last much longer.

She looked at Prince Omar and decided not to point out for him the significance of those ten formative years in Calgary. "I see."

"This method you have for teaching children to read. You developed this yourself?"

"Only partly. It's really a variation of the old phonetic system, which everyone over the age of forty in this country learned by. But it was thrown out and now they teach English as if it were Chinese—as though we had no alphabet, but only pictures depicting words. It's a terrible waste of an alphabet." She could feel the soapbox forming under her feet and forced herself to shut up.

"The princesses—" she noticed that he hadn't yet said "my daughters" "—can speak English quite well. But they cannot read. They read Arabic and Parvani and French very well, they are intelligent, but they say they cannot understand English reading. Is this the reason?"

"Well, without knowing who my predecessors were…" She shrugged.

"These children you taught—their mother tongue was not English?"

Jana nodded.

"What language was it?"

"Nearly any language you care to name." She smiled. "I can say *very good* in fourteen languages."

"*Khayli khoub,*" said Prince Omar.

Jana raised her eyebrows.

"That is how we say *very good* in Parvani, Miss Stewart. I hope you will have reason to say it to the princesses many times."

Three

A week later the royal party filled almost the entire first-class cabin of the small Royal Barakat Air jet. Only half a dozen seats were empty, one of them beside Jana, and so she read, and ate, and contemplated the amazing step she had taken, in lonely luxury.

Her parents had remained nominally opposed to this career move, even while secretly impressed by the thought of the Barakat royal family. Their opposition had faded quickly in the face of her determination. And as for Peter's—it had never materialized. Had he ever, Jana wondered, wanted to marry her? Or had it been, for him, the "thing to do"?

Someone slipped into the seat beside her, disturbing her train of thought, and she looked up from the book she had not been reading to see the old vizier.

She smiled a welcome, and they chatted about nothing in particular for a few minutes. Jana had been deeply impressed by the old man from the first time she met him. He had an air of humility that would make it very easy to underestimate him, she thought, and she was sure it would be a mistake to do so. Those calm black eyes saw into human motives, and she was a little afraid of him.

He chatted to her about her new charges, Masha and Kamala, and how tragically unnecessary their mother's death two years ago had been. If she had been taken to the hospital—but Prince Omar had been away, and in his absence no one had dared to take the responsibility.

Jana frowned. "It can't have been much of a decision to take a sick woman to a hospital!" she said.

"She did not want to go. No one had the authority to overrule her."

"You mean, no one would take the risk of defying a sick queen to save her life?" she asked in disbelief.

"Would you have done so?"

"Well, I hope I would have! My God, is the place really that protocol bound? What was Prince Omar's reaction when he got back? He must have been furious."

"He was very distressed indeed. But it was impossible to blame anyone."

Jana wondered why he was telling her this story. To help her understand the princesses...or the prince?

She said tentatively, "Was...was Prince Omar very much in love with his wife?"

The vizier smiled and lifted his hands. "Who can look into the hearts of men in such a matter?" he asked rhetorically, and Jana thought, *You probably do it all the time.* "He has said that he will not marry again."

Jana stared at him. "Are you—?" she began, but Hadi al Hatim was already slipping out of the seat, and with a friendly nod moved on up the aisle.

She puzzled over his motives for a few minutes. She had almost said, "Are you warning me off?" but it was ridiculous to think that anyone could imagine she had her eye on Prince Omar! He was as cold as—but then, what *was* his motive for telling her? She had too much respect for the vizier's capacities to think that he had spoken at random.

It was a minute or two before she thought to ask herself why she had asked the question. It was no business of hers if Prince Omar's heart had died with his wife.

Prince Omar stayed in his seat at the front of the cabin throughout the flight. People came and went around him, bowing over his chair, kissing his hand, handing him papers, staying to talk. Jana got up once to go to the toilet, which was at the front of the cabin. She passed by Omar's seat at a moment when he was sitting alone, going over some papers. He must have noticed her pass, because when she came out of the toilet, he looked up and called her name.

She obediently stopped in front of him. "Your Highness," she murmured.

It was the first time she had seen him since their interview at the Dorchester. She had been ruffled and irritated then, but now she was cooler, and behind the coldness in his eyes she saw a bleak look that she had not seen before. Or perhaps it was just because of what Hadi al Hatim had told her about the queen's death.

"I have only been out of England three hours and already I hear no English spoken," he said. "Sit and speak to me."

She thought how much more pleasant the command would have been if he had troubled to smile while issuing it, but the man looked grim enough for a hanging judge. She sat in the seat beside him, still uncertain about what was the protocol for such near contact with the monarch.

"Why *should* you hear English spoken?" she asked.

Looking a little surprised at the question, he said, "It is a language I have always wished to speak well."

"You sound pretty fluent to me."

Prince Omar shook his head. "No. Compared to my...my brothers, I have only a poor grasp of English."

"Then your brothers must be native speakers," Jana said with a smile.

There was no response. "One studied at a university in the United States, the other in France. In both places they had the opportunity to perfect their English."

"While you learned Russian?" she guessed, remembering what he had told her about his time in that country.

"Yes, I learned Russian. It was my father's thought that a small country should be able to communicate with the leaders of powerful nations in their own language and understand their culture."

"And I guess you can't really blame him for not knowing what would happen to the Soviet Union." True enough, but she supposed it wasn't much consolation.

"I do not blame my father in any case. But it was not—"

He broke off suddenly, and blinked at her, as though wondering why he was speaking to her so personally. "Well, it is not important."

"Where did you learn your English?" Jana asked quickly, and the impersonal question seemed to put him at ease.

"From my father's first wife. He married a foreigner. She learned to speak Arabic after she married my father, but she said that English was a useful language and she spoke to us only in English. It was my father's wish that we spend time with her."

"No wonder you speak so fluently."

His eyelids dropped in a brief negative. "When several people are speaking, I find it hard to follow. Very hard sometimes."

He was such a closed man it was hard to accept that the purpose of this conversation was really what it seemed on the surface, but Jana said it anyway.

"If all you need is practice—" she shrugged "—I'd be

quite happy to provide conversational English whenever you wish.''

She was prepared for a rebuff, but instead he fixed her with a look of surprise. "Will you have time?"

They had agreed that, as well as teaching the princesses to read English in formal lessons, she would supervise them at certain other times, so that they would learn spoken English as a part of their daily lives. But it still didn't amount to a full working schedule. "I suppose it depends on when you're free. We would have to organize it for times when the princesses are at other lessons or something."

"Yes," Prince Omar said slowly. "Yes, this is an idea I shall consider. Thank you."

"Didn't you have such an arrangement with previous English teachers?" Jana asked in surprise.

"No."

He was looking stiff and kingly all of a sudden, but she had seen behind that facade, however briefly, and she wouldn't let it put her off so easily. "Do you mean they refused?"

"The subject was never mentioned." He paused. "Only with you."

In the curious way that sometimes happens, the words rang with significance. The silence was broken only by the droning of the plane's engines as they looked at each other. Jana's heart pounded in her ears. "I see," she said at last, for something to say.

Just then Ashraf Durran came up to the prince, and a minute later Jana was back in her own seat, trying to figure out what, if anything, had just happened between her and Prince Omar.

At the airport in Barakat al Barakat, the party was met at the aircraft by limousines. Everyone stood around calling and shouting for a few moments, organizing the stowing of a mountain of baggage, and as Jana stood waiting by the car she had been directed to, she noticed that Prince Omar slipped away from the group and went striding across the tarmac alone. She watched him for a moment, until he arrived at a helicopter parked some distance away and began to check it over in a very professional manner.

As the convoy of cars pulled away, she heard the beating of metal wings, and watched out the window as the helicopter slid by above their heads and headed out over the desert.

The palace looked as though a genie had just responded to her wish for a magic castle. Arches, minarets, terraces, domes—all in white, blue and terra cotta—seemed to cascade down the sides of the rocky rise on which it sat, brooding over the city. The late sun was throwing a golden mantle over the whole horizon, and the desert glowed.

Behind, palace and city were encircled by the magnificent snow-peaked mountains that, in the distance, curled around the broad desert plain from north to east.

Jana rubbed her eyes and looked again. It hardly seemed possible that this would be her home for the next year—or more. She had spent ten years in the shadow of the Canadian Rockies, but this scenery was harsher and far more rugged. Not so picture-postcard scenic, but every bit as stunning to the senses.

She saw a helicopter landing pad as they swept up the curving drive to stop at the palace, but no sign of the black helicopter. Ashraf Durran came over and asked her to identify her bags, and a few minutes later, as they followed the servant leading them to her room, she took the opportunity to say as casually as she could, "Prince Omar did not return to the palace?"

"Ah, no. He had…other business to attend to. He will be away a matter of a few days, perhaps."

So he had not troubled to stay and introduce the new English teacher to his daughters. It was ridiculous to feel disappointed, and of course she didn't. But she found herself wondering where he had gone.

Her "room" turned out to be a beautiful apartment with a wide terrace looking east out over the desert. On her left, far away, the mountain range curved protectively around the desert; on the right she had a glimpse of the city and of a long, rushing, sparkling river.

The rooms were full of what seemed to Jana magnificent pieces of Oriental art: carpets and bronze jugs and miniature paintings and beautifully carved furniture and openwork shutters. Ashraf Durran introduced her to the woman waiting there.

"This is your personal servant, Salimah. She speaks English. Salimah, this is Miss Stewart."

"Hi," said Jana, as Salimah bowed and murmured more formal greetings.

"Salimah will help you unpack. Is there anything else I can do for you at the moment?"

"I would like to meet the princesses," Jana said. She would not meet the other tutors for several weeks. The princesses normally had a long summer holiday while the tutors returned to their homes.

He lifted one hand and smiled. "Salimah also will arrange that. If you wish, she will show you around the palace. But first, perhaps, you would like a cup of tea or coffee or other refreshments. I leave you in good hands, Miss Stewart."

With that, he bowed and was gone, his air an indescribable mixture of formality, humility, and arrogant nobility that left her breathless.

When the door closed behind him, Salimah smiled. "Shall I help you unpack?" she asked, leading a resistless Jana through a broad doorway into the bedroom, where a huge double four-poster bed was draped with beautiful greens and blues, and a magnificent wardrobe was covered in the tiniest mosaic work Jana had ever seen.

An hour later, having unpacked, showered and drunk a deliciously cool fruit drink, Jana told Salimah, "I would like to meet Masha and Kamala now."

Salimah bowed. "Yes, Miss. I will take you to their nurse."

She led Jana through such a series of halls and rooms that Jana thought she would never find her way unguided. She noticed the curious fact that, like the stately homes of so many of her parents' friends, there were discoloured rectangles on the walls. Several of the glass-fronted cabinets that mostly held antiques and treasures were empty, too, or had empty spaces where something had once lain.

In Britain the cause was always the same—death duties that forced the sale of family heirlooms. She wondered what had put Prince Omar under financial pressure.

"But where are the princesses' rooms?" she asked, as they turned yet another corner.

"They are beside their nurse's room, of course."

Beside the nurse's, but a mile from the English teacher's. Jana raised her eyebrows over the arrangement, but Salimah was not the person to argue the matter with.

Umm Hamzah, the old woman who, Salimah explained, had been the personal servant of the princesses' mother and was now their "nurse," was a short, stocky, dark-skinned woman with thick, grizzled grey hair hanging in a braid down her back, a wide unsmiling face, and dark suspicious eyes. She had about half her teeth remaining, and her wrinkled face had seen the burning sun of many, many summers.

She greeted Jana in Arabic, and then explained through Salimah why it was not possible just at this moment for her to meet the princesses. Later it would certainly be more convenient.

Jana nodded. "Where are the princesses now?"

"I think they are having a bath, Miss," said Salimah uncomfortably.

Jana smiled at Umm Hamzah and asked exactly when she should return.

"Someone will bring the princesses to your room later, Miss," Salimah translated.

But no one brought the princesses to her room later. Jana was served a delicious dinner in her apartment, watched the sun's rays fade and the sky darken, watched the lights of the city come on, watched the fat, heavy moon rise and sparkle on the dark river, and went to bed with a book.

For two more days it was not "convenient" for Jana to meet the princesses. Salimah grew more abashed and embarrassed with each explanation, and the old nurse less voluble, as if victory in this senseless battle made her less and less polite.

"The princesses are sick, Miss Stewart," Salimah offered, her eyes on the beautiful glazed tile floor. "They are in bed."

"That's all right, take me to them in bed."

"La, la!" shouted the old woman, waving both her twisted hands as Salimah made the suggestion, and shouted at Salimah.

"She says it is very…easy for someone else to get it," Salimah translated.

"Contagious," Jana supplied automatically. "That's all right." She had gotten the picture long ago, but she still wasn't sure how to deal with this hostile old woman. "I never get bugs, I'm not worried. Take me to them."

Again urgent shouts and waving hands greeted Salimah's words. "They are too sick to be seen by anyone, Miss."

Jana felt her blood starting to boil. "Well, in that case," she said carefully, taking a shot in the dark, "I must call Prince Omar immediately on his mobile phone and urge him to return to the palace instantly. He is on urgent business, but he would not like to be absent at such a dangerous time. I will call him now."

If the old woman called this bluff, what could she do, Jana wondered? She didn't even know if Prince Omar *had* a mobile phone, let alone the number. But she saw Umm Hamzah's jaw clench and her eyes widen in alarm as she spoke, and knew she had won. Jana wondered how much impact this old woman had had on her queen's decision not to go to the hospital when she was so ill, and how frightened she was of Omar's displeasure.

Half an hour later the princesses, healthy, clean and neat, were brought to her apartment by a servant. The two pretty little faces gazed at her in fascinated alarm as the introductions were made, and as soon as they were alone, Jana asked, "What is it?"

"Are you the devil's handmaid?" asked Masha, her eyes wide.

Four

Jana kept her calm. "No," she said, "I'm not. Did some-one tell you I was?"

Masha, her eyes dark, nodded speechlessly. She was the elder by only about eighteen months, Jana knew, and ex-cept for a little difference in height, the two perfect little faces could almost have been twins.

Jana was pretty sure she knew who the *someone* was. "She made a mistake," she told them calmly. "Don't you know what my name means? My full name is *Jahn-eh Ros-han,*" she prompted, pronouncing it as Prince Omar had done.

They both frowned in thought. "Soul of light!" shouted Masha, and Kamala repeated the words in childish excite-ment, as if she had discovered them herself.

"That's right. So how could I be the devil's handmaid?"

It wasn't all that convincing, as logic goes, but it seemed to impress the princesses, who stood there nodding, relieved smiles on their faces. "But your name is Parvani," Masha told her gravely after a moment. "Nana doesn't speak Parvani, only Arabic."

Nana was Umm Hamzah.

"Oh, well, that's how she made the mistake, then," Jana said pityingly. "Poor Umm Hamzah. She just didn't know."

They were satisfied with that, and Jana decided to leave it there. But she understood that Umm Hamzah had declared war, and she intended to keep her guard up.

Over the next few days, Jana spent time getting to know the princesses. Umm Hamzah went on making efforts to restrict Jana's access to them, but with Salimah interpreting Jana simply said that it was Prince Omar's command, and would allow no excuse to get in her way.

She soon became as determined to get the girls away from their grim nurse as the nurse was to keep them away from the foreign devil. Umm Hamzah was a superstitious, uneducated, illiterate woman, and some of the stories that Kamala and Masha relayed to Jana made the hair lift on her scalp. She was sure the old woman's preoccupation with sin, death and the devil was not good for them, and she did her best, in a mild, unconfrontational way, to counteract Umm Hamzah's influence.

Both the little princesses already spoke good basic English, and so, although she gave them formal lessons in reading, almost anything she did with them could be considered an English lesson. So they played games, and went for walks, and fed the sheikh's horses apples, and watched the desert tribeswomen washing clothes in the river, and swam in the palace swimming pool.

"This water is not so…good the water at my father's special place," Kamala, searching for the words, said nostalgically the first time they swam. Jana was a good swimmer, and she was already devising water games that would teach them English and how to swim at the same time.

"Not as nice as the water at your father's special place?" she repeated. "Where is that?"

Both girls sighed longingly. "In the mountains," Masha told her. "The mountains of Noor," she explained further. She pointed, and Jana turned to look at the mountains in the distance. She saw a stretch of desert, and then the tan-and-pink-coloured foothills, and above, those snow-capped, beautifully inhospitable peaks.

There must be a kind of country residence up there, and why not? Summer down here on the desert would have been close to unbearable on some days without the cooling system in the palace. Jana's skin was already a warm shade of tan after only a few days in the sun.

"Do you go there every summer?"

Both princesses shook their solemn little heads at her. "No," Masha said, sighing again. "Two times we go there. It is very beautiful, Jana. Very beautiful. We had such lovely time."

"We saw our father every day. It was not like here at the palace. Here we do not see Baba."

"He spoke to us and took us riding and showed us many things."

"He did not go away and leave us during the whole time."

They were so pathetically eager to tell her about it, so sad at the loss of their joy. Her heart ached for them. Poor little princesses, who never had their father to themselves.

"Perhaps your father will take you there again," Jana suggested, wanting to comfort them.

The girls smiled, lifted their shoulders and sighed. By which she understood that they had given up hope of such happiness.

"Is the house still there?"

"Oh, yes."

"Baba is there now," said Masha.

Jana was startled. "Is he?"

"We saw the *halikuptar*. When he goes in the *halikuptar*, he goes to the lake," Masha said, as if it were a fact of nature. "But we do not go."

"Shall I ask him about it?" Jana asked. She was curious about the place, and about why there was apparently to be no repetition of holidays that the children remembered with such pleasure.

They stared at her as if she had transmogrified into a magician as they watched. "Can you?" Kamala breathed.

"Oh, Jana!" Masha said.

"I can try. I'll mention it, first chance I get," she promised.

From that moment on, she could do no wrong. Devil's handmaid? They knew from first-hand experience that Jana was an angel.

Prince Omar returned two days later, a fact she learned because the sound of the helicopter drew her out onto a terrace that had a vantage point over the helipad. She saw him disembark, and her heart kicked with satisfaction. For her as for his daughters, it seemed, the palace was incomplete without their father.

She remembered their conversation on the plane, and waited to be summoned to Prince Omar's presence. But the hours and days followed one another and she got no summons.

Then one hot evening, after the princesses were in bed, Jana went to the pool for a late swim as was her custom and found Prince Omar there, alone, swimming up and down the length of the pool in a fast, strong crawl. After a momentary hesitation, Jana stripped off her robe and dived in.

When she had done a few more leisurely lengths she stopped at the deep end, and found that he was sitting on the edge not far away. The water was still streaming down his skin, so she guessed he had only just pulled himself out of the water. Maybe he hadn't realized till now that she was even in the pool.

"Good evening, Your Highness," she said, blinking water from her eyes.

"Good evening, Miss Stewart."

"I hope you don't mind me breaking in on your solitary use of the pool. I often swim here in the evening, and no one told me—"

"It is quite all right. I told no one of my intentions."

His voice was remote, and she thought he did mind. Since he was the sheikh and could have whatever he commanded, she wondered why he didn't just tell her to go.

In the next moment, he had agilely leapt to his feet. He was clearly going to leave.

"Your Highness," she called softly, but her voice had an urgency on the hot desert air.

He stopped and turned to her. "Yes?" he asked, as graciously condescending as any fairy-tale monarch in his throne room.

He had a fabulous body, she noticed by the light of the moon. Slim muscular thighs, strong arms and chest, tall and lean. There were one or two scars. His hips were narrow, his swimsuit small and snug, a racing suit, and she couldn't help noticing, since he was practically standing over her, how generously he filled out the fabric between his thighs.

It wasn't really like her to stare at a man's sexual equipment. Jana dragged her eyes up to his. "You've been in the palace for several days, but you haven't asked me for any English conversation."

"Oh!" he said, and frowned. "Yes, I had…forgotten."

She was sure that he had not forgotten, that he had changed his mind for some reason, and a curious kind of panic overtook her. "Well, if you're free now, I have time. Maybe you'd like…"

She faded out. She pulled herself out of the water and

stood dripping before him, and they stood staring at each other, without recognizing how much time passed.

Her figure was graceful and supple, and very sexy, with long smooth lines at shoulder, waist and hip, and beautifully delicate ankles. She was wearing a plain white one-piece that cupped her full breasts like a pair of masculine hands, and her nipples pressed against the thin wet fabric, visible even in the near darkness.

Omar thought of his ancient ancestor, who had been so proud of his wife's beauty that he hid his best friend in a closet so that he could see her as she disrobed and know how fortunate was the king in his wife. He had always thought that ancestor a fool, rightly deserving his wife's wrath when she discovered the ruse. But now he found himself wondering if his ancestress had perhaps been as beautiful as this. If so, no wonder her poor fool of a husband had been so besotted.

But he had no intention of trying to bed his daughters' English tutor, he reminded himself, no matter how lovely she was. Omar did not allow sex to complicate his life. He chose his sexual partners carefully and made sure they knew exactly what they could expect if they submitted to his proposals. This woman was much more valuable—because rarer—as English tutor to the princesses than she could possibly be as mistress, a role that many women could fill.

Her skin glistened in the light of the moon, just rising now in the black sky. Her red hair looked sleek and dark, her white swimsuit glowed, her full lips smiled at him. It was a pity that he had not foreseen that he would want a woman tonight, and ordered that his current mistress be at the palace.

They stared at each other wordlessly in the warm night, and at last Jana felt her cheeks growing hot.

She turned and bent, then straightened and slipped her arms into her cotton robe and tied the waist while he

watched. Then she stood absently gazing out at the desert
in the moonlight. The world seemed full of shadows and
magic, and stars in a profusion she had seen nowhere else
were spangled all over the night sky. Jana sighed.

"How beautiful this is," she whispered. "It's magic,
isn't it? It's no wonder people fall in love with the desert."

Omar wrapped himself in a voluminous striped robe and
tied the cord at the waist with a little snap. His jaw tightened at her words, but she was looking at the distant dunes
and did not notice. "Do you think so?"

The tone of his voice startled her, so full of cynical unhappiness that she turned and blinked at him. "Don't
you?"

"I have never loved the desert," he said flatly.

She was surprised. She had always imagined that those
born in the desert loved it. She watched him for a moment
under the starlight. At their feet the pool, softly lighted
underwater, gurgled and splashed. "What do you love,
then?"

He gave a bark of laughter. "You speak as if everyone
must love something."

"A person would have to be very hard not to love some
part of the natural world," she said mildly. "So hard they
couldn't be called human."

His eyebrows moved. "I love the mountains. I am only
half an Arab, Miss Stewart. My mother's people are mountain people, the love of the mountains is in my blood. Even
the sea I love better than the desert. Nevertheless it suited
my father to leave me that third of the kingdom which is
mostly desert."

Jana was silent. They stood side by side, looking out at
the night. As the moon rose higher, the snow on the mountain peaks glowed white, with purple and black shadows
drawing dramatic curves and lines over their surface.

"Why?" she asked.

"I have never known." He was talking to her as he had

never talked to a woman, not since he was eighteen and unhappy and had tried to talk to his wife.

"Do you have no coastline, no sea access, no mountains in your territory?" she asked after a minute.

"The mountain range to the north is mine. Those mountains ahead of you fall within East Barakat. The border between Central and East Barakat lies in that defile..." He moved behind her and pointed over her shoulder to where a dark slash seemed to have been cut through the mountain range by an angry sword. "The River Sa'adat rises there. It defines the eastern and southern borders of the principality. Through that river my people have access to the sea, but we have no coastline."

She felt the heat of his body behind hers, and his arm beside her ear radiated warmth. She felt rather than saw that his left hand came up as if to rest on her left shoulder. It hovered for a moment, and then touched her, and Prince Omar directed her to turn as he followed the distant course of the river with his pointing finger. It glinted in the white moonlight, which was becoming brighter as the moon climbed the sky.

"Without that river this land would be nothing."

The heat of his hand burned through her thin robe as Jana obediently turned to follow the thread of rushing water until, closer to the city below, its true size became more apparent. "We watched the women washing their clothes in the river the other day," she said. "It was like something from the Bible. I bet women have been doing that for thousands of years."

"Many of my subjects live in such primitive conditions," he said, and the bitter tone in his voice again made her turn to gaze at him. She was startled to find his face so close to hers. "It is my goal to change this during my reign."

"Automatic washing machines aren't civilisation, Your

Highness," she observed gently. "They are only technology. There is a difference."

He stared down at her, so close she could smell the mix of his shampoo and some other odour that was perhaps sheer maleness. "Do you think so?" he asked.

She wondered what it was they were really talking about. She managed to keep the thread, but her mouth moved on words that seemed meaningless, as though the part of her that spoke and the part of her that looked into his eyes were two separate women.

"The women we saw were cheerful and hardworking. To an outsider, your subjects seem as happy as many in the West who have the advantages of technology. Masha told me some of them were telling their little children stories as they worked, stories of the tribal past and of kings, she said, and sometimes stories about animals and magic. If you put electricity in every home, that will eventually be replaced by television. Are you sure it will be an improvement?"

He straightened and turned her to face him. He felt how quick the sexual urge was in him tonight. And something else.

"What are you saying?" he asked, gazing into her eyes.

She wasn't sure. She was too much under the spell of Prince Omar and the night. She was trapped by his dark gaze, and it would be a miracle if she could remember her own name. Jana swallowed and stared into his eyes, and felt his fingers tighten on her shoulders.

A servant entered the pool area behind them and spoke. The prince instantly let her go and turned.

"*Baleh,*" he replied, and imperiously signalled a dismissal. When the servant had disappeared, he asked, "Have you eaten dinner, Miss Stewart?"

"I usually have something in my room a little later," said Jana.

"It would be convenient if you would eat with me. Then

we can speak English together,'' said Prince Omar, in a return to that haughty voice too used to command.

"Sure, Your Highness,'' she said, with a deliberately casual air.

"Ask your servant to bring you to my private dining room in half an hour,'' he ordered.

Jana pursed her lips. There was a limit, after all. "My hair is wet, Your Highness,'' she said softly. "Shall we say forty minutes?''

His chin jerked a little in surprise. People did not challenge him, although certainly, as it was only a request, he reminded himself, she had a right to do so.

Prince Omar bowed graciously. "Forty minutes,'' he agreed.

"See you then,'' said Jana, and waggled her fingers at him as she disappeared.

Five

"Good evening."

His private dining room was a half-covered terrace looking out towards the desert and the mountains from nearly the same angle as the pool. The floor was decorated with glazed tiles laid in intricate oriental patterns, the walls were white, as were the pillars that supported the roof. Climbing plants and flowers were everywhere, and a table was laid in the centre with silver and crystal. Flames under glass provided the lighting.

Prince Omar stood at the stone balustrade, smoking. He was wearing a dinner jacket, and he looked as elegantly mysterious, Jana thought, as the enigmatic character in a James Bond film whose affiliations are unknown, but who may well turn out to be the enemy. He was staring out over the landscape when the door was opened, but had turned immediately to greet her.

"Good evening," she replied, and moved over towards

him. She was dressed with care for her first dinner with her princely employer, in a flowing deep green silk-and-cotton unwaisted calf-length dress over draped trousers, and a long gauzy matching scarf. The dress had a stiff, high collar, but was cut open in a curving triangle to reveal the lightly tanned skin above her breasts, which the scarf, its tails flowing out behind her, only partially concealed.

She wondered if he appreciated the anomaly of the fact that while he had dressed in Western fashion, she was in Eastern dress, but she was nervous of him and did not point it out.

Her red hair she wore in a sophisticated coil at the back of her neck. Some curling tendrils had already escaped around her cheeks, and her bangs were slightly flyaway, as usual. On her ears and wrist she wore shimmering jade-and-gold drop earrings and a bracelet, on her feet, delicate leather sandals.

Prince Omar nodded as he watched her approach, but did not speak. Jana stopped at the balustrade beside him. She seemed to feel his presence even at a distance of several feet. Was that what they called the aura of power? she wondered. A servant approached with a drinks tray and Jana studied the choice for a moment.

"He will mix a cocktail for you if you prefer it," Prince Omar said. He was smoking a black Russian cigarette, and drew a gold cigarette case out of his pocket to offer her one.

"Thank you. May I have a vodka martini, very dry?" Jana said, and dropped her eyes to the cigarettes as the prince relayed her request.

Like most teenage girls, she hadn't been able to resist the lure of something so temptingly forbidden as cigarettes, and had spent a month or two in various garages and alleys with schoolmates on their lunchbreaks, enjoying the illicit pleasure until it dawned on her that she didn't really like the taste all that much. She hadn't smoked since then.

But one thing she had never tried was one of these elegant black cigarettes, and after a momentary hesitation, she accepted one. She put it in her mouth and leaned a little into the flame that Prince Omar held for her, protecting it against the light breeze with his other hand. She was abruptly, sharply aware of how erotically symbolic the little ritual was, drew breath on a little gasp, and coughed gently as the sting of the unfamiliar smoke caught her throat.

He felt his loins stir again as she slipped the cigarette between her full red lips and accepted the touch of flame at his hands. "They are a little strong if you are used to American or English tobacco," Omar murmured. He dragged on his own and restored lighter and case to his jacket pocket. He turned back to his study of the desert.

Not only the desert. Jana was surprised to see, at a distance below them, the soft lights of the swimming pool. "Actually, I'm not used to any tobacco." She smiled. "I don't smoke."

Had he *known* that she usually swam at that time of evening, then? The thought that he had gone to the pool with the deliberate idea of bumping into her made her heart kick.

He smiled sideways at her, a slight frown hovering over his strongly marked eyebrows. This woman was always catching him off guard. "No? Why do you smoke this one now?"

Jana laughed and accepted the martini from the servant with a murmur of thanks. "I suppose because I always wondered what a black Russian cigarette tasted like, but never got a chance to find out. And to keep you company."

He rarely smoked in public, but still he had endured his share of lectures and stony looks from various Westerners, women especially. But this woman seemed entirely unpredictable. He wondered in what other ways she might be unpredictable. "And how do you find it, the taste?" he asked, but it seemed to him that the question was about something very different.

"Very strong, I think. I like the aroma, but I wouldn't dare to inhale," Jana confessed.

Her words, too, seemed charged with double meaning, but not one he could decipher. Prince Omar laughed. It was a sound she hadn't heard before on his lips, and it was a deeply, sensually attractive experience.

The cigarette really was strong. Her teenage decision held good even for black Russian cigarettes.

"Do you smoke these regularly?" she asked, suppressing another cough.

The prince smiled at her. "A man who smokes regularly has given up his self-control. I prefer to exercise self-discipline in my pleasures."

She felt the heat of her own thoughts in her cheeks. She couldn't think of anything to say. She turned away to the landscape.

They gazed out at the moon and the mountains and the nearly endless desert for a few moments.

Jana sighed deeply. She didn't think she had ever experienced anything so luxurious as this night, and her spirit seemed to expand. She hadn't realized before how grey her life had become, living and working in a deprived area, fighting a losing battle for so long. "You have to admit there's something very hypnotic about it," she said quietly. "It exerts a terrible fascination."

She meant the desert. Prince Omar turned his head and found that he was locked in her gaze again. *A terrible fascination.* Was that what he felt? If so, where would it end? Should he fire her and send her away immediately before he was more tempted?

Another servant entered and asked permission to serve the hors d'oeuvre, and Omar led Jana to the table.

Something very aromatic was offered to him, but with a gesture he indicated that she was to be served first, and the waiter slid a plate containing two small rounds of what looked like stuffed aubergine before her and then put another in front of the prince.

He watched as she slipped the fork between her lips. "Mmm!" she crooned, and the sound cut through him. "This is delicious! What is it called?"

Omar put a question to the server, who bowed and replied. "This is *Imam Bayaldi*," Omar said. "It means 'the Imam fainted away.'" He wondered if a man, a lover, had ever made her faint away. He wondered if he could. He would like to try. "Have you tasted it before?"

"I've certainly eaten something by that name in Middle Eastern restaurants in London, but it didn't taste anything like this!" Jana said. "Now I see how it got its name!"

A half smile hovered on the prince's lips. She was a strange mixture of enthusiasms. He said, "There are those who say that the Imam fainted, not from the taste, but because his wife told him how much olive oil went into the making of it. The Imam perhaps not being very rich."

Jana laughed delightedly, her head arching back to offer him a view of her slender neck and throat. "Is olive oil so expensive?"

"Not for me. My brother's groves supply all my needs," he said dryly.

The waiter popped a cork. Jana's eyes smiled with pleasure. "Champagne?" She licked an errant drop of olive oil from her lower lip, and he suddenly realized how close he was to losing his resolve. Through sheer will he got a firmer grip on his imagination.

"To welcome the new English tutor," he said coolly. When the glasses were filled he lifted his towards her. "I hope you enjoy your time here, Miss Stewart."

His voice was cool and had the odd effect of reminding her that this wasn't a dinner date but an English lesson. Suddenly the spontaneous pleasure of the situation seemed to drain away. Jana picked up her own glass and saluted the prince. "I hope my English lessons prove satisfactory, Your Highness," she said.

"Let us talk about economic subjects, please," he said, and it was clear that, however exotic the surroundings, business would be business. "I have some meetings to attend later this year, and my vocabulary is deficient in that area."

"Probably more extensive than mine, Your Highness," she muttered dryly.

With a fork halfway to his mouth, Omar stopped and stared at her. "What did you say?"

"I wouldn't bet a whole lot on my chances of being able to improve your economics vocabulary, unless you get the *Financial Times* and would like me to read it to you."

He raised his eyebrows. "How do you mean?"

"I don't attend trade talks, you know, I teach children. And your grasp of English is a lot better than you seem to believe."

He looked remote and haughty.

"However, if you have a specific agenda, you'd better tell me what it is. What exactly will you be talking about at these negotiations?"

"Some of the Barakat Emirates' trade agreements must be renegotiated in early autumn."

"What do you export?"

"Oil, precious stones, fabrics, clothing, ornamental glassware, ceramics, charcoal, pottery, other crafts," he began. "Furniture, charcoal braziers, and we have support industries manufacturing for the electronics industry."

"Not bad for a small country," Jana responded in surprise.

"My father used the oil money in the seventies to create small local industries run by each clan chief on the old pattern of the crafts guilds. He insisted that we would sell no raw materials except for oil. Although many thought him a fool, his strategy has proved to be economically very sound. Our pollution level is low, we have high employment while maintaining tribal strengths—that is why the cities are small, we have not uprooted the tribes from their environment.''

Jana found it interesting. For half an hour she listened and provided the odd question while Prince Omar expounded on the economic state of his kingdom.

Suddenly he stopped. ''But this is no good!'' he exclaimed. ''You haven't corrected me!''

Jana, absorbed in what he was saying about a tribe whose women had made their own traditional woven cloth the rage as a furnishing fabric in the West, so that they had had to make peace with a hostile neighboring tribe in order to enlist their workers, blinked.

''Haven't *corrected* you?''

''My English, my use of the language!''

''Your Highness, everything you have said so far has been fully comprehensible.''

''But not always correct!''

''Not always perfectly correct. So what?''

He stared at her. She laughed, she couldn't help it. He watched her lips move over her neat white teeth.

''What is the point of language, Your Highness? To be correct in itself, or to communicate ideas?''

''Language must be correct.''

''On that basis, a wheel which is a perfect square is better than a wheel which is round but a little irregular. Which one will take your cart farther?''

He was silent, gazing at her. ''Do you teach the princesses from this point of view?'' he asked at last.

''The princesses,'' she said deliberately, ''are not engaged in trade talks.''

''Do you correct their errors, Miss Stewart?'' he repeated firmly, as though she were being evasive.

Jana pursed her lips, thought better of the angry retort that came to her lips, and then explained her technique for dealing with the princesses' grammar mistakes.

"Errors in speaking should be corrected," he said flatly. "Or how can they—"

Jana put down her fork with a little snap. Probably it wasn't protocol to interrupt a prince, but Jana was too hot to think of that. "I remind you that you agreed you would not interfere in my teaching techniques!" she said, her chin set and her gaze direct.

"To correct errors is not a 'technique'! How will they learn good English from bad if they are not—"

"The princesses are well under the age of puberty and there is every chance that they can become fluent speakers with sufficient practice. You can't be always correcting mistakes in a second language! It's counter-productive," Jana said.

He stared at her for a long moment of arrogant surprise. "Why do you mention puberty?"

"Because before puberty children seem to have second-language abilities that adults do not. They can become as good as native speakers."

"And for me, not?"

"You make a few small mistakes, which possibly you will never be able to correct entirely. They do not affect meaning, and so—"

"What mistakes?"

So they were back where they started. She realized that it was an issue with him. Reason was not going to alter his position very much.

Jana sighed. "You sometimes leave out *the* or *a* when it is required."

"You must explain these rules to me. And what else?"

Jana shrugged and left it to another time to explain there was no rule to cover every circumstance. "Every now and then a mistake with verb tense. You say, for example, 'was doing' instead of 'have done,' or the other way around."

He gazed at her, nodded once, and thoughtfully ate another mouthful of food. "What do you suggest?"

"I suggest, Your Highness, that you stop worrying about your errors, which may improve anyway over time, and concentrate on building your vocabulary in areas where you need it."

He regarded her steadily for a moment.

"I also suggest more recreational use of English, perhaps with your daughters. If you're comfortable with expressing yourself in private life, you will almost certainly be more comfortable in a formal setting."

"Do you think so?" Prince Omar looked surprised but not sceptical. Unbidden there came to his mind the words that he would like to use to express himself to her.

"Yes, I do." Smiling, Jana attacked her food again. It was a lamb casserole with Eastern spices and herbs, utterly succulent. "Your daughters have mentioned to me several times that you took them for holidays by a lake in the mountains," she said casually.

"Yes?" His eyes were shuttered.

"Have you thought of taking them for a holiday again?"

"Not to that place, Miss Stewart. Why do you ask?"

She dropped her eyes and felt the heat rise to her cheeks at the snub. "Because they enjoyed it so much and I think it would do them good."

He blinked at her with such arrogant astonishment that she almost apologized for the question. Clearly here was a prince not used to being challenged.

"Are you a psychologist, Miss Stewart?"

She sensed that he was angry, but if so he was hiding it behind coldness as sharp as frostbite.

"I'm a human being, Your Highness! Are you really so Western that you think no one knows anything about human beings unless they've taken a degree in the subject?" she demanded hotly.

He bowed, stony faced. "Having asked you to correct me, I am in no position to complain if you do so."

Jana pressed her napkin to her lips, but her eyes glinted at him, full of humour.

He couldn't resist. His lips twitched. "Nevertheless, the desert is dangerous, Miss Stewart, and Lake Parvaneh is a long way."

She didn't believe that was his reason for not taking them. There was so clearly something else behind what he was saying. But she nodded.

The next course was a pastry full of butter and honey and about as fattening as anything ever made, Jana thought, but she could not resist a taste, and once she had tasted, she could not resist eating it all. She sighed luxuriously as the memory of their heated words seemed to fade, and the magic of the desert night closed in around the balcony again.

"I hope you will join me again for the evening meal," he said, as two little cups of strong coffee were placed in front of them.

"Yes, of course," she said. "When?"

"Tomorrow night," he said, knowing himself for a fool. "It will be good for me to be forced to express myself in English every day." He might as easily have said, *good for me to test my restraint in your presence.*

"Do you want me to come here every night?"

"On those evenings when I am here." And even then he knew that he would be away less often than before.

Six

"**Y**ou have had the fortunate opportunity to observe at close hand the different political systems of Canada, the United States and Great Britain," Prince Omar said.

"I suppose so."

"Explain them to me, please."

Good God. "They aren't all that different, really. Canada and the U.S. both have systems derived from the English parliamentary system." She made a stab at outlining the three systems, wishing she had studied harder in her high school modern history. "Will you describe the Russian system to me?"

"The system which I learned was the Soviet system," he said. "It is no longer relevant. Shall I make an opportunity for you to visit the parliament in Barakat al Barakat?"

From being served on a tray in her apartment, Jana had moved to these delicious dinners on Prince Omar's magical

terrace, accompanied by conversations that, at Prince
Omar's request, ranged over every topic...except the personal. He wanted to talk about economics, politics, geography, history, religion, literature...but he did not want to
talk about his two daughters or their obsession with Lake
Parvaneh and yearning for another holiday with their father
there.

Or, of course, about the curious mixture of pleasure and
pain he felt in her company, or how, almost against his
will, he watched her swim each night from the safe distance
of his balcony, and struggled with himself not to join her.

He knew their conversations were often awkward and
strained, but it did not occur to him that the reason was
that he was not saying what he wished to say to her.

She smiled at him. When she smiled, her lower eyelids
curved upwards in engaging little arches that gave her face
an impish and yet deeply sensual expression. He felt how
easily such a woman might undermine a man's resolve, and
tightened his self-control in such moments.

"I might have a little difficulty following the argument,"
she pointed out.

Tonight she wore a plain yellow sundress with narrow
straps over her brown shoulders. Her lipstick was a burnt
orange colour that reflected certain lights in her hair. Omar
thought how easy it would be to stand up and walk around
the table to kiss those full, smiling lips, and frowned. "Of
course I will assign an interpreter to go with you. You will
find it interesting, I think, and it will give us subjects for
discussion. My vocabulary will gain in the area of politics
and government."

Jana put down her fork. "Your Highness."

His eyebrows went up in polite enquiry, and Jana almost
gritted her teeth. After that first night, when his guard had
slipped by the pool, he had never been anything except a
prince and her employer wishing to improve his English.
Sometimes she had an almost irresistible urge to challenge

him, to say something that would shake him, get an unguarded response from him. Common sense usually made her wary of treading on the tyger's tail.

Not tonight. Somehow, she had reached the end of her tether tonight. The end of her tolerance for these rigidly impersonal conversations and his rigid control.

"Miss Stewart?"

"I find your daughters much more interesting at the moment than your parliament. Could we discuss them for a moment? Your vocabulary might gain a little in the area of human feelings."

His curving lids came down to hide his expression from her, a sign of regal displeasure she had learned to recognize. Through sheer determination she was growing resistant to it.

"Miss Stewart, you should discuss the princesses' welfare with their nurse, Umm Hamzah," he said.

"Umm Hamzah is exactly what I wish to discuss," Jana returned firmly.

The old nurse's jealous possessiveness was becoming a serious problem. Kamala and Masha were becoming more and more attached to Jana, and the stronger Jana became in the princesses' affection, the weaker Umm Hamzah felt her own hold to be. She could not understand the concept of adding a new person into the affections. As far as she was concerned, by as much as they loved Jana, she herself was exactly that much less loved. As a result the old woman was determined to maintain her grip by any means possible. Every day she invented a string of reasons why Jana should not be with the girls, why the girls had to do this or that rather than study English. And Jana knew she talked to them about her in a way that made them very uncomfortable. She was sure that part of the reason they so fantasized about the house at Lake Parvaneh was an unconscious need to get away from the strained atmosphere.

"This is mere jealousy," Prince Omar said now, when

she tried to make him see the extent of the trouble. "It will certainly disappear over time."

Jana was sure that he felt that half of the problem, half the jealousy, was Jana's. He did not believe what she told him of Umm Hamzah's machinations.

"Umm Hamzah speaks to the guards, and then I am prevented from taking the princesses down to the city for shopping, for example. Today I spent an hour arguing before we were allowed to go out."

"The job of the guards is to protect the princesses. They naturally wished to enquire…"

"Look, Your Highness, she is telling Kamala and Masha—and I don't know who else!—that I am the devil's handmaid! She fills their heads with tales of bandits who will come and get them if they don't do everything she wants, or if they go outside the palace with me! How long do you expect them to be able to stand that? Their loyalties are divided, and it is very hard on them. And on me!"

"She is an uneducated woman," he responded impatiently. "She believes that *any* foreigner is the devil's handmaid, and she thrives on rivalry because it gives her life an interest. It is the fate of women of her generation. I can do nothing about Umm Hamzah. That is what she is. Do not bring to me tales of arguments between women! You are here to see that the princesses will be able to rise above these foolish rivalries of the harem, not to engage in them yourself. That is why I have them educated. That is your job."

"It is not my job," she contradicted angrily, "to defend myself against constant charges that I am in league with the devil! It may be a ridiculous situation, and I'm sure the concerns of mere women are well beneath your royal masculine notice, but this is very hard to deal with! And your daughters are feeling a lot of stress! So am I!"

He felt the thunder of his own blood. It was a mistake

to allow himself to show or feel anger in her presence. But it was already too late.

"My daughters must learn to deal with stress! There will be more stress than this when the time comes for them to convince the tribes that they should rule!" he said angrily. Then he clamped his jaws together. He sensed the rush of other, quite different feelings released in anger's wake, and was even angrier with her for disturbing his control.

It was the first time that she had ever heard the words "my daughters" pass his lips. Jana sat silent for a moment. His face had grown shuttered and closed. "How soon exactly are you expecting that day to come?" she demanded.

Omar blinked. "Pardon me?"

"You're not even forty yet!" she burst out. "Are you expecting to fall off your horse tomorrow? The princesses are children, and they have had plenty of unhappiness and stress to deal with already in their young lives! They do not need any more!"

He smiled grimly at a joke of his own. "I am thirty, Miss Stewart. But a man can die at any time. That is why we say, *mash'allah*. Whatever God wills."

Thirty! Jana looked at the silver threads in his hair and wondered if it was grief at his wife's death that had put them there. Her heart gave one hard, heavy beat.

"If you died tomorrow, do you really think the unhappiness Umm Hamzah is causing Kamala and Masha would give them an ounce more strength in proving themselves to the tribes?" she asked, refusing to be diverted.

"Miss Stewart, the happiness or unhappiness of the princesses is not your concern. Their command of English is. Perhaps if you will confine yourself to that, you will have less trouble with Umm Hamzah."

"Right," she said flatly, and waved away the servant's offer of coffee. "Well, I no longer wonder why it is you can't keep an English tutor. I resign as of now."

It was only half bluff. She really couldn't stand what

was going on, and if Prince Omar wouldn't stop it, she knew it would only get worse.

His face remained impassive, but his eyes glinted with steel. "You are not in a position to resign. You have signed a contract to remain for one year."

"Sue me for damages," she said rudely. "You can't keep me here against my will."

Even as she said the words she felt a little thrill of horror. How did she know what he could or could not do? He was Prince Omar ibn Daud ibn Hassan al Quraishi, monarch of all he surveyed.

He looked at her, and she saw the first glimmer of real feeling in his eyes since that night when they had swum together. She saw the flames, but she could not tell what the feeling was. Anger? "I will keep you here," he promised softly. "For the full duration of your contract."

Her skin shivered over her whole body. If he decided to make her his prisoner, if he cut her off from the world, who would know? It might be a month before anyone at home became seriously alarmed, and how long after that before the issue could be forced?

"Like hell you will!" Jana stood straight up so that her chair fell backwards. A lackey appeared at once from some dark corner of the terrace, but was instantly waved away by the prince, and at a further command left through a door, leaving them entirely alone.

Omar moved behind her and lifted her chair onto its feet. "Sit down, Miss Stewart," he growled.

The air was tense with expectation as he stood close over her, and then, moved by deep impulse, his hands reached out and enclosed her bare upper arms. "Please sit down."

She supposed it was because they never touched that the touch was so electric on her skin. She was a natural toucher, but she never used those confiding little pats during conversation with the prince, never kissed or hugged him the way she did with her friends. So there must have been some kind of buildup, she supposed. It made her knees weak, and with seeming obedience, she sat.

After a moment, he lifted his hands from her arms and both of them breathed deeply, as if they had not breathed for the past few seconds. Prince Omar returned to his own seat, looking as remote as ever.

"Within the harem, no man has any power, and a king is a fool if he thinks otherwise. However, with my guards, it is another matter."

He rang, bringing the servant back into the room. A quick command was followed by the arrival of a beautiful antique silver tray bearing paper, pen, a silver inkpot, a silver matchbox, and what looked like a stick of red crayon.

With a calligraphic flourish that left Jana breathless with admiration, Prince Omar wrote several lines of Arabic on a sheet of paper and then appended a signature. When that was finished, he lighted a match, picked up the red crayon, and began melting it over the paper.

When there was a globule of red on the paper, Omar drew off his gold seal ring and expertly pressed it into the sealing wax. Then he picked up the document, waving away the tray, and handed it to Jana.

She sat for a moment gazing at it in astonished admiration for this ritual from another century. She was holding in her hand what could only be a royal permission, with the king's seal on it!

She looked from the beautiful Arabic writing to the inscrutable face of the prince. "What does it say?"

"That you are not to be impeded in your duty of educating the princesses in the English language," he informed her shortly.

"Thank you, Your Highness," she said.

"You must of course always be accompanied by an armed guard when you take the princesses beyond the palace walls," he said.

"Of course." She laid the document carefully beside her

handbag. Suddenly a little plan in the back of her mind, like an ember that has been blown on, puffed into life.

The plan was this: to run away with the princesses to the house at Lake Parvaneh and give them a holiday there. They would have half their dream—the lake, but not their father's company and undivided attention. She would leave a note for Prince Omar telling them where they had gone, and begging him not to send anyone after them.

Of course it was a foolish, impulsive plan. If he got very angry or believed that she was kidnapping the girls, he might send the police or army after them, and she would be sent home at once—if not executed, Jana told herself with grim humour. But Jana hadn't yet learned to curb her impulsive nature. This plan seemed to be the only solution open to her.

Kamala and Masha had a picture of the house by Lake Parvaneh where they had spent such a happy time. They were not in the picture; it looked much older than that to Jana. It had been taken in the sixties or seventies, she thought. It was a black-and-white shot, showing the house and part of the lake with the mountains in the background. The girls were adamant that it was where their father had taken them, and that it belonged to him.

The house was not like any house Jana had ever seen. She could feel herself falling under its spell as surely as the girls had done, simply through the photograph. Her longing to see it became almost as strong as Kamala and Masha's.

For all her impulsiveness in conception, Jana was very organized in execution, and she laid her plans very carefully.

First, she set about gathering information as unobtrusively as she could. Her first source was Salimah, the only other palace employee who spoke English with whom she came in daily contact. Salimah was Jana's conduit into palace life and gossip, and a valuable adviser on Barakati customs. They had long ago dispensed with the formality of "Miss Stewart," and treated each other as friends.

It was Salimah who had told her that Prince Omar had become estranged from his brothers after the death of his wife, though no one knew exactly why. It was just at that time, too, that Nizam al Mulk, the Grand Vizier to all three princely rulers of the Barakat Emirates, who might have been able to effect a reconciliation, had died. Since that time, because of the rupture, there had been no Grand Vizier of the Barakat Emirates.

So Salimah was already used to Jana's interest in and curiosity about everything. When she drew Salimah into casual, disguised discussions about travel and roads in the desert, about how far away the mountains were, she learned such useful things as that the road that followed the course of the river out of the city led to the mountains, and that Lake Parvaneh was on a tributary of the river.

Of course she couldn't confide her plan to Salimah. She was almost sure that Salimah would keep the confidence, and even help her, but if there was going to be trouble, it would not be fair for Salimah to suffer Prince Omar's displeasure. So she never gave anything away. She never mentioned the house, or the princesses' desire to go there.

Jana began to teach the princesses geographical terms. She got them to draw maps of Central Barakat, labelling everything in English, including Lake Parvaneh. She chose the best of their maps and kept it safe.

There were several vehicles for use by the palace staff, both for personal and work use. Jana started asking for the Land Rover whenever she went out—not only to get used to driving it on the desert roads, but also to accustom the garage staff to her use of it. She made sure to take it out late at night, too, always flashing her royal warrant if challenged by a guard. She would park by the river for an hour and return.

She took the princesses on lunch picnics down on the river, or out in the desert to the picturesque ancient ruins dating from, so it was said, the time of Alexander. They were always accompanied by a guard on such occasions, and Jana gave a lot of thought to the problem of whether it would be possible to take a guard when the time came. But how could she confide in one? And how could she take one with them if she did not?

The princesses told her that their father had bought food from the tribe in the valley that surrounded the lake, but Jana couldn't count on that. So on every shopping expedition she carefully added to a growing hoard of nonperishable supplies. She also bought one or two pieces of equipment, such as a camp stove.

Since she could not pack any of the girls' clothes without Umm Hamzah discovering the fact, she had to buy them each a summer wardrobe. There was plenty of Western-style clothing in the shops, and she bought them the basic minimum of shorts, T-shirts and swimsuits, jeans and sweaters for the cool evenings. She bought similar clothes for herself. She packed all these things and hid the cases and boxes in a locked cupboard in her apartment.

At last everything was ready, and the time of the full moon came. "I've got a surprise for you!" she told the princesses at lunch that day.

Jana's surprises were always wonderful, and the two girls clapped their hands in delight. "What surprise?" they chorused. "What surprise, Jana Khanum?"

Khanum was the title that Prince Omar insisted they use with her when she had made it clear that she would not agree to their calling her Miss Stewart and he would not agree to their calling her Jana. The expression, she knew, had a certain formality, but the sound was almost poetic, and soon it had become a term of affection, their own private nickname for her. No one else used it.

"Tonight we are going to sleep on my balcony and study the stars."

If they were thrilled then, they were thunderstruck with delight later when, after an hour spent lying on mattresses staring up at the magical night sky and repeating the names of the constellations, she told them what treat was really in store for them.

"You are taking us to the lake?" Kamala breathed, her eyes wide and black with amazed excitement. "Oh, Jana Khanum! When do we go?"

"In a few hours. So you must both go to sleep now, because we have to drive at night."

Masha nodded wisely. "So that the bandit Jalal won't see us," she said.

The bandit Jalal was the bogeyman whom Umm Hamzah used to scare the girls into obedience. He would come to their beds and snatch them away if they were not good little girls. Or he would steal them from the desert if Jana took them too far.

She had found it impossible to convince them that there was no such person, and had come to the decision that the less attention she paid to the idea the better. So now she merely said, "It will be very hot driving across the desert during the day, that's why we have to go at night. I will come and wake you when it's time to go. And remember we will have to be *very* quiet, because everyone will be sleeping and they won't like it if we wake them up, will they?"

"I was sick once in the night," Kamala told her. "Umm Hamzah was angry when we woke her, but when she saw how sick I was, she forgave me."

Jana smiled at the ease of it all. "Well, you aren't sick now, so we'd better not wake up Umm Hamzah! We'll only talk in whispers, okay?"

They nodded like two little nodding dolls. "Okay, Jana Khanum."

In spite of their excitement, they fell asleep quickly. Jana gently closed the sliding door so that they would not be disturbed by the noise she made as she began making preparations to leave.

Seven

"**D**o you think the attempt will succeed?"

Jana had been lost in a reverie, but now she awoke as if he had thrown cold water in her face. She brought her gaze to focus on Prince Omar's face with wide-eyed horror. "Pardon?" she whispered. How had he known? What had she said to give it away? What would he do?

He looked at her with his eyebrows slightly raised in surprise and suddenly she almost laughed with relief. She wasn't sure what was being attempted, or who was doing it, but one thing was certain—he was not talking about her projected flight tonight. Still, it unnerved her. He was so damned quick on the uptake.

"Oh—I suppose so, I don't know. What's your opinion?"

She nervously fingered her wineglass. The full moon crept up the sky behind the mountains and glinted in Prince Omar's eyes. She had chosen the night of the full moon to give her the best light on the desert road, but she wished His Serene Highness did not seem so much of an eagle tonight. *Eagles have better vision than humans,* she thought, *and I bet you have sharper eyes than most.* She gazed absently out at the road in the far distance, where in the clear air faint pinpricks of light arced over the desert. If anything disturbed his sleep and he got up, he would see the lights of the Land Rover for miles from here. Would he recognize the machine? Would he guess?

"You are not concentrating, Miss Stewart," he said dryly. "I have just said what I think. What is it that pre-occupies you?"

Heat rushed to her cheeks. Playing for time, she lifted her glass and sipped. "I'm just a little tired tonight," she lied. She was wide awake: not only had she slept for a few hours this afternoon in preparation, but adrenaline was now pumping through her system.

She looked at Prince Omar and thought that probably he would fire her for tonight's escapade. She realized she would be very sorry never to see him again. She enjoyed these nightly meetings with him, even if he did keep the conversation ruthlessly impersonal. She would miss them, just as she would miss the desert nights, and the heat, and the sight of the mountains, and the people of Central Barakat...there was a lot she would miss. Even in the short time she had been here, she had grown attached to the country.

"It has been very hot," Omar murmured. He had watched her swimming, length after length, knowing that the sultry heat was filling her body, as it did his, with a sensual energy that had no outlet. She had stood up out of the water and raised her hands lazily to her hair, sweeping it back; her head had fallen back, her eyes had opened and she had seen him on the terrace above. She had neither waved nor smiled, but turned abruptly away. He knew women. He was not mistaken in the response he sensed in her. What a fool he had been not to accept her resignation when she offered it. He must send her away soon.

Not yet.

"Very hot," she agreed. "Salimah tells me that in the old days, the days of your father, this palace was never inhabited in the summer, that the whole court moved up into the mountains. Why don't you do that nowadays?"

He smiled grimly, and she knew she had touched a sore spot. "Because the summer palace now belongs to my brother Rafi. He must live there in winter, just as I must live here in summer. It is how my father's will divided the kingdom."

"But what about the house at Lake Parvaneh?"

He shook his head. "That is not big enough to hold my court."

"But you could go there yourself. You could take the princesses. I am sure this heat is not healthy for them."

"Miss Stewart, you have said this before in another way. I have answered you. If the heat of the day is too much for the princesses, do not take them outside during the day. The palace is cool enough."

Not for him. There was a breeze now, but it was hot. *The kind of hot wind that maddens a man,* Omar thought. *Especially if he is already mad with desire.*

"Is Baba coming with us?" Masha whispered a few hours later as the two princesses excitedly dressed in the jeans, T-shirts and jerseys Jana had bought for them. They had never worn such clothes, and they considered them as exotic as Jana did the *shalwar kamees* she had worn to dinner tonight with Prince Omar.

"No," she said, because if they spent the next week in anticipation of their father's arrival and he didn't come, they would be very disappointed.

Jana paused. *She* would be disappointed. Five minutes ago she had slipped into his study and left a letter on his desk, telling him where they had gone. Would he come after them himself?

Slowly she opened the door, and all three of them crept barefoot along the darkened passage towards the garages.

They met no one. With military precision the two princesses lay down with their pillows on the back seat of the Land Rover and Jana covered them with a light blanket. "Silence, now!" she cautioned, worried that they would pop up to greet the guard if he challenged her going through the gates. "Go to sleep. I don't want to hear a sound."

Four or five times in the past two weeks, Jana had taken the Land Rover out at midnight. At first the guard had been astonished, but she always returned within the hour and he had grown used to it. He believed she must be meeting a man, but he had no instructions to stop her.

Tonight he didn't even get up as she stopped at the gate, merely pushed the lever from where he sat and lifted his hand in response to her wave. Then they were through and moving down towards the city.

Jana wondered when Prince Omar would see her note. "I have taken the princesses to Lake Parvaneh for a vacation," she had written. "I have told no one, and so you will have to make explanations this morning about why we are missing. I am sorry to do it this way, but I was afraid you would forbid the trip if I asked you." After some thought, she had written a postscript. "I know the princesses would be very happy if you joined us. We will return in a week."

The road turned east and began to run along the bank of the river. Now it was just a matter of steady driving, watching out for drifted sand and potholes in the moonlight. By dawn she counted on being in the foothills.

Once she glanced back over her shoulder to where the palace glowed white and mysterious in the moonlight. She wondered if Prince Omar was asleep or awake. Perhaps he was still sitting on his balcony, smoking and thinking.

She wondered if he was watching the lights of the Land Rover. They were almost the only vehicle on the road.

Sayed Hajji Omar Durran ibn Daud ibn Hassan al Quraishi crushed the piece of notepaper between his fingers and cursed aloud.

"Damn her!"

It gave him some relief to vent his feelings, and he cursed softly and repetitively for another few seconds, his eyes flashing with emotion, before his jaw clenched tight again.

It was not unusual for him to be in his office at an early hour, but it was only just past five and he was not often up so early unless there was something particularly absorbing his attention. He was not sure why he had come here this morning—it had been his intention to ride—but thank God he had.

The palace wasn't really stirring yet. Staff would soon be at their tasks. In the summer everyone preferred to work early and late and rest in the middle of the day, but it was unlikely that anyone had yet noticed the absence of the princesses and their tutor.

Omar stood for a moment in thought, then slipped silently out of his office and up the stairs.

Ashraf Durran came awake with the first touch of his sovereign's hand on his shoulder. "Sire," he said softly, using the title of a warrior to his commander in that moment, as if the unexpectedly early wakening had raised old responses. Then he blinked and took in his surroundings. His room in the palace, not a tent on a battlefield of Parvan. "Omar," he said then, swinging smoothly to his feet. "What's up?"

Omar showed him the note. Ashraf read it in silence, then lifted his eyes to Omar's. "Is she crazy?"

"She has not been told. I did not think it necessary."

"Who went with them?"

"That is what we must find out. First, that they are actually gone. Second, whether she took a guard. Third, what time they left. And of course without arousing comment."

"You aren't going to raise the alarm?"

"What would be the advantage, except to advertise that the princesses are at this moment crossing the desert virtually unprotected? No, we must keep it quiet."

Ashraf nodded. "I will go and talk to the guard." He was already tossing his clothes on and after a moment stood straight. "I'll pretend I can't sleep."

Omar nodded at the good sense of this. "Find out who went with them, and what pretext she gave. She planned carefully. Last night the girls slept on her balcony—to watch the stars!" He cursed himself for his own blindness and strode out.

Ashraf came to his office ten minutes later.

"Ali is on duty and has been all month," he reported. "Miss Stewart often goes out in the Land Rover at about midnight and returns in an hour or so. He thinks she has a boyfriend in the city."

Omar's jaw tightened. "She does not have a boyfriend in the city," he said flatly. Ashraf raised an eyebrow at him. "She is a careful, meticulous planner. What happened last night?"

"She left as usual at just after midnight. She has not yet returned. No one was with her. No guard was requested to accompany her. No doubt the princesses were in the back of the car, hidden."

"The fool!" Omar exploded with fury. "Midnight! Allah, they may already—" He bit back the words. "Ashraf, here is what I plan. I will take the helicopter now and follow them. She cannot be making more than fifty miles an hour, I will catch them in two or three hours—if they are still on the road. You meanwhile tell the staff that I have taken my daughters and the English tutor with me on a holiday. They will understand the reasons for secrecy. Send Ali on some trip to keep him from talking. If all is well, I will pick them up, proceed to the lake and signal you in the usual way.''

Ashraf frowned. ''Omar, I'm coming with you!''

Omar shook his head. ''No. I can take no one else into my confidence in this. You must be here to see that everything is accepted without comment. All being well, we will stay at the lake some days and then return.''

''And if there's a problem? If they have been captured? If you yourself are taken?''

''You will hear soon enough. It may be that this is the moment when I settle accounts with Jalal the bandit. I hardly care who is the victor, Ashraf. Take care of my daughters, try to maintain their inheritance for them, if it should go against me. I appoint you regent until Masha's maturity. The warrant is here, signed and sealed.''

The two men wordlessly shook hands. The prince clapped his hand on Ashraf's shoulder and went out.

It had been a longer, harder drive across the desert than Jana had expected. Sand had drifted onto the tarmac in many places, treacherous at night, and her shoulder muscles were weary with the struggle to keep the vehicle on the road when the sand grabbed the wheels or they hit one of the numerous potholes that studded the miles.

She had stopped once, at a gas station in a desert town, to get gas, drink some coffee from the thermos she had brought and stretch her weary muscles. She had had to awaken the owner, but he had made no objection. Kamala and Masha had slept through, but they would be waking soon. The river, and the road following it, had changed direction several hours ago, and now was headed north north east, she thought, up into the mountains. It meant the rising sun was not in her eyes.

The desert was bleak and inhospitable here, and she was not surprised that Omar did not love it. There were many desolate rocky outcrops, the surface sand was grey and gravelly, and underneath, the earth was stony and hard. She saw bleak ruins from time to time in the distance, testaments to the futility of man's attempts to conquer such terrain.

But ahead were the foothills, and the promise of green valleys. The land had been climbing very gently for the past twenty miles. Jana glanced at her watch. Almost eight o'clock.

"Are we nearly there, Jana Khanum?" asked a sleepy voice from the back seat.

"We'll stop for breakfast soon, and after that it'll be awhile longer. See, we're just getting into the foothills now."

"Jana Khanum, I have to pee."

"So do I."

"So do I," said Jana. "All right, we'll stop for that now." She glanced in the mirror. There was no one else on the road for miles, so she simply pulled up near a small rocky outcrop and all three of them got out and relieved themselves behind it. She gave them a drink of water, let them run around for a minute, and just as they returned and were climbing in, she heard the unmistakable, rhythmic thud of hoofbeats.

A savage-looking dark-haired man in a white burnous was coming across the sand towards them on horseback, and although Jana was sure the savage looks were nothing more than a cultural perception, a little thrill of fear zipped up her back. She bundled the girls into the Land Rover and, without doing their seatbelts up, jumped in herself and pushed the automatic door lock.

"Do your seatbelts up," she told them calmly, but she certainly didn't feel calm. The man had pulled up a few yards away and was staring at them. "Masha, help Kamala with hers, I'm starting now."

He made no attempt to approach any nearer, but as she drove past she saw him staring first at her, then at the two princesses, and last of all at the license plate before he wheeled his horse, kicked its flanks cruelly, and galloped off back the way he had come.

Masha and Kamala watched in silence out the back window until he disappeared from sight. "I think that was Jalal the bandit," Masha told her sister calmly.

"Will he come and get us?" Kamala asked, her eyes wide with dread.

In spite of herself, Jana put her foot down and pushed the needle up to sixty. "There is no Jalal the bandit!" she told them firmly. "That's a story Umm Hamzah made up so that you would be good girls."

She glanced in the mirror and was surprised to see both girls nodding their heads with vigorous conviction. "Yes, there is a Jalal the bandit! Baba told us all about him when we were at the lake before! He is a very bad man!"

Jana frowned. "*Baba* told you about him?"

"Yes! He said Jalal the bandit is a very bad man who wants to take his kingdom away from him and would like to take *gerugahn* so that Baba would have to give him some of his land."

Electric shivers were coursing through her blood. *"Gerugahn?"* Jana repeated, from a dry throat.

"Yes, I don't know the word, it's when you…you take someone and put them in a bad place until someone gives you something."

"Hostage," Jana supplied faintly. "Prince Omar said that the bandit Jalal would want to take you hostage?"

"Yes, he said we are never, never to go out into the desert alone, but must always have a guard with us, and we are never, ever to run away without telling someone where we are. I promised,'' Masha said solemnly. "Kamala promised too, didn't you, Kamala?''

Her sister nodded.

Jana's heart was pounding so hard she was almost deafened. "What else did he tell you about the bandit?''

Now, when it was too late, Masha was a mine of information. "He said that the mountain tribes hate Jalal the bandit, and they are our friends, so if we are in the mountains we are safe. If we are in trouble we must say to a mountain tribesman in Parvani, 'I am of the house of Omar ibn Daud the Durrani and I ask your help.' They are sworn always to help us. Baba and his army and Companions fought with the Parvani people in their war, and many of the mountain men went with him, also.''

Jana felt physically sick, but she managed to smile and make her voice smile, too. "And does he live near here, this Jalal the bandit?''

Another nod. "I think so, Jana Khanum, because Baba did not say those things to us when we were at home, but only when we came to Lake Parvaneh. I forgot all about it until we saw that man. It is good that we are with you, Jana Khanum,'' Masha said, with a sigh of total trust.

"Yes, it's a good thing you're with me,'' Jana repeated. She put her foot down as far as she dared. The engine roared, taking them towards the mountains and safety. She wondered if the license plate of the Land Rover carried some code that citizens of the country would recognize as being from the palace. Or perhaps the bandits simply knew all the palace vehicles.

Far off to the left, in her mirror, she could see a cloud of dust in the desert. She had never seen a troop of horsemen galloping across the desert before, but that was what it looked like to her.

Eight

Omar pushed the helicopter as hard as he dared. To gain time, he had come directly across the desert rather than following the road. He would pick up the road at the foothills, because she could not possibly have travelled further than that, and then track back along it till he found signs or until his gas ran out. If they had been captured, it was likely that the Land Rover would be left at the scene.

At the very least she would find some way to leave him a sign.

If they had not been captured he would force her to stop, and he would take them all aboard.

He was filled with a cold, vibrating fury. He had had time—hours—to hone his anger to diamond hardness. Every movement he made in piloting the machine was precise, wasting no effort, exactly as his words would be when he found her. His eyes scanned the desert beneath him and the sky ahead with unsparing precision. If they were there he would see them.

Then he lifted over an outcrop and saw ahead of him everything he had feared and hoped to see, in a tableau: the ribbon of highway beside the rushing river running from left to right across his view, the Land Rover, roaring flat out towards the mountains, and nearer to him, almost directly ahead, a high choking whirlwind of dust which had at its epicenter a cluster of horsemen. The horsemen were converging on the Land Rover at nearly the same angle as he was.

He was still at a distance. They would not have heard the sound of his approach yet. Without taking his eyes from the scene, Omar reached behind his seat with one hand and lifted the small green Uzi into his lap.

If he could see them now, Jana thought as she hit another pothole with brain-numbing, muscle-tearing force, their father would be proud of the princesses. They had reacted to this terrifying turn of events with calm and courage.

"Will the bandit Jalal capture us?" Masha had asked once, as they watched the menacing dust cloud approach nearer and nearer.

"He might," Jana had told them. "If he does, we will pretend that we only speak English. You must pretend not to understand him unless he speaks in English, can you do that?"

"Does the bandit speak English?"

"I don't know. Whatever he says, don't answer him. Let me talk. If we pretend that you are not the princesses, he might let us go."

"All right," Masha said calmly. "Kamala, if the bandit comes, we will pretend that we are Scottish, like Jana Khanum. We will pretend that she is our mother. Do you think that is a good idea, Jana Khanum?"

"A very good idea," said Jana. "I can't talk anymore, Masha, darling, I have to concentrate on driving."

"All right," said Masha calmly. "I will make plans with Kamala."

Thereafter the girls had muttered together for a few minutes, and then Masha said, "We will be silent now and help you concentrate, Mommy."

A curious little kick assailed her heart, and then Jana forced her attention back to the road. The foothills were rising around them, but she had no idea how far into the mountains Jalal dared to enter. It would be at least two miles before they began to be protected by the hills, and meanwhile the horsemen were gaining perceptibly. She could only go so fast. If she went off the road they were lost for certain.

"Baba!" someone screamed. "Look, look, it's Baba!"

Jana almost leapt out of her seat. "Where?" she cried, because she couldn't take her eyes off the treacherous road for a moment.

"In the *halikuptar!* Look, look, Masha, it is Baba! He is going to kill Jalal the bandit!"

He laid a line of bullets down in the sand behind the horsemen to announce his presence, and in another moment his shadow passed into their line of vision and he was coming over them, flying low. He hoped she would have the good sense to keep heading for the hills.

Directly above them now, he laid another line of warning bullets in front of them. Some of the horses panicked at the double onslaught of the low-flying helicopter and the bullets digging into the sand, and they reared and began to whinny, breaking up the charge.

Several of the men did what he had expected, and pulled rifles out of their saddles. He pushed for height, but they were experts and were already taking aim. Omar sprayed them with another stream of bullets, wrestling with the helicopter controls with one hand.

He gained height. The Land Rover was already out of range of all but one horseman. The others were fighting to calm their horses in a melee of men, beasts and choking sand. Only one galloped toward the Land Rover. A man of determination, then, but Omar had already known that. He pushed the machine to scud along the sky after the horse and came up alongside him.

The horseman looked up, and he looked down. They met each other's gaze for an almost imperceptible moment, and again he raised the Uzi in one hand. Jalal, guiding his horse with his knees, did the same with his rifle.

There was a curious moment when each man had the other in his sights, and each man shifted his aim. Jalal to aim at the helicopter motor, Omar to aim at the horse. It hurt him to kill the fine-looking animal, but a strange reluctance to kill the man had invaded his soul.

The two men fired at the same time, and at the same time the horse went down and the helicopter engine faltered. Then the helicopter roared past and the downed horseman was lost to Omar's sight.

In another moment he had passed over the Land Rover, too, his engine missing badly. Trust the bandit to hit something crucial in the last second.

He was in the foothills now, battling with the big machine, knowing it would not land gently. He could not crash land in the road, because then the way would be blocked to the Land Rover and Jalal might still come on. He veered off over the rocky landscape, where he knew safe landing would be all but impossible. He flew on, hoping for one clear stretch to land on, fighting to keep the machine up till he found it.

"Is Baba hurt?" Masha asked calmly.

It was the first anyone had spoken for several minutes.

The princesses had watched the ground-to-air battle without a word, gripping each other's hands, breathing in gasps, but calm. No screaming, no pleading had crossed their lips.

"I don't think so. It's the helicopter. The engine has been hit. He is looking for somewhere to land," Jana said, with a calm she did not feel. She did not say that to be dragged away from the road was a catastrophe in the rocky landscape. Her heart was pounding in sickening, painful thuds as the helicopter vanished from their view.

She looked back. Far behind them now the horsemen were in a ragged group on the desert floor, some horses and men lying in the sand, some standing. The last man, the one who had chased them longest, stood over his struggling horse and fired one shot. The horse went still. No one would follow them now. Around the next turn, out of sight, Jana put her foot on the brake. When the Land Rover came to a halt she jumped out and vomited bile into the ditch.

Then she stood straining her ears, listening to the sound of the helicopter's engines in the distance. She heard the increasingly distressed whine, heard it cough, and fire, and then, sickeningly, heard it cut out altogether.

A moment later she heard the ugliest sound she had heard in her life. Up until this moment the ugliest thing she had ever heard was her parents arguing, long ago when she was a child, but now and forever it would be the sound of the metal and glass of Prince Omar's helicopter smashing into rock.

It took her half an hour to reach him. There was no smoke, no black column of death to tell her where to search, and for that she had to be grateful. But each minute, each second of that time was a torment, wondering whether she had missed the site, whether he had crashed out of view of the road. But she had to drive on. She decided, if she did not find him en route, to leave the princesses at the house and then go out to search. If she climbed up high, she might see the wreck.

But he had just missed the road, coming down between two sheer rock faces onto a small clearing. The rotor blades glittered in the sun, and the twisted machine lay on its side halfway down a steep grassy slope, with the river at the bottom. He had narrowly missed a tree.

With a cry of mingled fear and triumph, Jana leapt out of the car and scrambled down the grassy slope towards the big broken machine, sobbing and praying all the way.

He was not behind the controls. Jana leaned helplessly, hopelessly against the shattered glass bubble and dragged in a hoarse, heaving breath. "Where is he?" she cried to the heavens. "Oh, please, where is he?"

Her fear was that he had been thrown out before the crash and that his beautiful, perfect body was smashed and broken against the rocks. Or that he had fallen into the river…

"Jana!"

She heard the faint cry, and whirled and cried desperately, "Omar? Omar? Where are you?"

Then she noticed what she should have noticed before: the brush of red on a rock, as if a bloody hand had rested there. Her breath coming in sobbing gasps, she followed the signs down towards the river's edge, terrified of what she would find.

"Here," he called, his voice sounding stronger now at close range, and in the next second she saw him. She ran and slid the rest of the way, frantic with relief and fear.

He was half lying on the riverbank, leaning against a high outcrop. There was blood on the ground under his thigh, and the black denim of his jeans was soaked with it. He had torn off his shirt and made a tourniquet to stop the bleeding from the ugly gash. Blood covered his forehead and cheek from a wound above his temple. But he was alive.

"Omar!" she whispered, falling on her knees by his side.

He opened his eyes and stared into hers. *"Janam,"* he said. He lifted up his hand to her cheek, and uncontrollably, she turned her face and pressed her lips against his palm. It was cold. Her heart quailed.

"Omar, Omar, thank God I found you!"

"Yes, *Mashouka,"* he murmured. "You found me. I was afraid you would not."

His eyelids were heavy, he looked half asleep. "You must take me to the lake, *Janam,"* he said. "Can you do that?"

"Yes," she whispered.

His hand touched her cheek again, and then he lost consciousness.

They reached the house on the lake at last. Jana sat for a moment at the wheel and felt gratitude flood up inside her with such intensity she could hardly contain it. The princesses, crammed together into the front seat, were filled with an emotion too strong for words.

"The lake! The lake!" Masha whispered, but that was all.

Prince Omar, lying propped up in the back, awoke, raised his head, saw the water, the house, heaved a sigh, muttered, "Well done, *Janam!"* and slipped back into unconsciousness.

She had wanted to turn around and drive back to civilisation, to the palace, to the city where there were hospitals. But apart from the risk of taking Omar so far in his condition, there was the spectre of Jalal. Surely there were more in his band than the few who had chased them. Even though she was afraid Omar had been delirious, she could only obey him, go on to the lake and hope that there might be a village nearby with some basic medical care, and someone who would carry a message to the palace.

She was terrified for Omar. The gash in his leg was horrible, but it was the wound in his head that was the unknown factor. She was almost totally ignorant of medical things, and knowing nothing, Jana feared everything. Was his skull fractured? Had a blood clot formed? Was his brain even now swelling from the blow? Was his neck broken? Perhaps she shouldn't have moved him at all, let alone dragged him up that slope? Yet he might have bled to death if she had left him there by the river while she went for help.

Someone was fishing on the lake. As soon as they arrived he started rowing to shore, and now, as Jana and the two little girls stepped out of the Land Rover, he raised an arm and shouted a greeting that carried faintly to them across the water. Masha and Kamala began jumping up and down crying, "Baba Musa! Baba Musa!" with the delight and relief of those who recognize an old friend who can be depended on.

"Who is Baba Musa?" Jana asked, as they waited for the old man to beach the rowboat.

"He is looking to the house for my father, Jana Khanum," Masha explained, losing her English a little under all the terrors and stress of the past few hours.

"He looks after the house for Prince Omar?" Jana asked, and breathed another prayer of gratitude.

"Yes, Jana Khanum."

"Tell him that your father has had an accident," she said.

As the weatherbeaten, white-haired man came up to them, smiling to reveal a lack of every other tooth, she saw that he was not as old as he looked at first glance. The teeth and hair were misleading, and he was probably not much over fifty.

The two girls were calling and crying to him, patting his arms and jumping with their mingled anxiety and pleasure in the meeting, bubbling over in a language she recognized as Parvani, not Arabic. Immediately they drew him over to Jana and she heard them introduce her as "Jana Khanum."

Jana smiled and extended her hand, and Baba Musa took it in his own rough-skinned grasp and spoke a greeting.

"Jana Khanum, Baba Musa says hello," Masha said.

"Hello, Baba Musa," said Jana, and he nodded his head. She turned urgently back to Masha, because there was no time to lose.

"Masha, will you tell Baba Musa that Prince Omar is wounded and ask him to help us carry him into the house?" Jana asked, and after that the child acted as interpreter between the two adults. Baba Musa, exhibiting a strength amazing for his size, carried Omar into the house and laid him on the bed in a room that was clearly Omar's habitual bedroom, then helped Jana undress him and examined his wounds. They put a makeshift bandage around his thigh, but left his head wound alone.

Jana worriedly muttered the word "doctor," and Baba Musa repeated it, nodding vigorously, as if he understood.

"He is going down the valley to find the doctor," Masha translated as the old man left. "He will be back soon."

Omar hadn't regained consciousness. This frightened her, but it was possible he was actually sleeping. Jana had no first aid training. She did what she could, bringing some warm water and gently washing the blood from his face and hands without disturbing the wound.

Then she sat beside his bed, wishing she knew what to do. After a few minutes, she reached out to slip her hand over his wrist and took his pulse. It was fast but strong, and she supposed that was good. She took comfort from the warm pulse of life that seemed to flow through him now. At the river, when she had found him, he had felt so cold.

"Mashouka," he had called her. She had thought him delirious, thought he was confusing her name with Masha's. But now, suddenly, she remembered him saying,

"Mashouka means *beloved* in my mother's tongue," and her own heartbeat was strong and fast, thudding through her temples.

Was it possible? She stared down at him and tried to quell the sudden surge of feelings that coursed through her.

Then, because there was nothing else she could do, she knelt by the bed, still holding his hand, and prayed. "Please," she whispered. "Please, please let him be all right," and she pressed her mouth against his hand as tears streamed down her cheeks.

He stirred, and she glanced into his grey face. "*Janam, do you pray for me?*" he muttered, and was immediately out again.

It was less than an hour before Baba Musa returned. Jana looked up from her post by the bedside with a smile of relief. "*Doktar awmadeh,*" he said.

"Oh, thank God!" said Jana. A woman had come in with him, carrying a cloth bag, who she supposed was his wife, healthy and strong, with flashing black eyes, a salt-and-pepper braid not unlike Umm Hamzah's hanging down her back, wearing the same kind of well-worn, stained, quilted vest as Baba Musa, and *shalwar kamees*. Around her head was a colourful scarf, also not very new.

She marched purposefully towards the bed, speaking to Baba Musa over her shoulder. Jana looked to the doorway. No one else came in.

"Where is the doctor?" Jana asked. Baba Musa smiled and nodded, understanding only one word.

"*Doktar Amina doktareh khayli khoubi ast! Khayli tond awmad!*" he told her.

Meanwhile the strange woman had picked up Omar's other wrist and was staring down at his face with serene concentration. While Jana watched in total horror, she bent closer over his head wound.

"Masha," Jana said faintly, "ask Baba Musa where the doctor is."

Masha stared at her. "This is Doktar Amina from the village, Jana Khanum. She is a very good doctor, I have heard Baba say so."

"Oh, my God!" breathed Jana. She sat in shock as the old woman bent attentively over Omar, listening to his breathing, opening his eyelids to stare into his eyes, and performing other little medical rituals that Jana had never seen before, now and then asking Masha a question.

"Doktar Amina says that Baba's head is not broken, Jana Khanum," Masha said, and in spite of herself and her distrust of the woman, Jana sighed.

She had tried to get Masha to leave, but Masha had resisted.

"Baba would say it is my duty to stay, Jana Khanum," she had said.

Doktar Amina unwrapped the makeshift bandage and thoroughly examined the thigh wound. She turned to the bag she had dumped on the floor and pulled out several bundles wrapped in fabric.

To Jana's amazement, the first one opened to reveal what looked like a lot of little black thorns. Then there was a curious odor, and a second parcel was unwrapped to reveal a mass of what looked like greeny-black stringy mud.

Jana couldn't believe it. Was the woman actually going to put this horrible mess on a wound? She was no better than a witch doctor!

"No!" Jana said loudly, stepping to the side of the bed and confronting the woman over it.

Startled, everyone turned to stare at her. "No," she repeated. "He needs a real doctor, and proper medication, and drugs to fight infection! You are not putting that filthy concoction on him!"

The old woman calmly turned to Masha for clarification.

"What is the matter, Jana Khanum?" the bewildered child asked.

Jana heaved a breath and gazed into those wide, trusting,

but worried eyes. How could she explain to Masha without frightening her? She glared at the old woman across the bed and the body of Omar. The black eyes were twinkling at Jana. And now Jana was struck by the fierce intelligence of that tolerant, amused gaze. The old woman laughed and made a quick comment to Baba Musa, then turned to Masha and said something.

"Doktar Amina says that you should not be frightened just because she shows you something you have not seen before," Masha translated.

"Tell Doktar Amina—" Jana began furiously, but she was interrupted from an unexpected source. A hand closed over her wrist, and she turned with a gasp to find Omar with his eyes open, looking up at her.

"Do not interfere, *Janam*," he said softly. "Doktar Amina knows what to do."

Nine

With the princesses' help, she unloaded all the supplies and cases from the vehicle, and put them away in the kitchen and the bedrooms. The princesses chose the room they had slept in before, at the top of the house, and Jana took the room next to Omar's, with which it shared the large jutting balcony overlooking the lake. The house, she found, was furnished in a pleasing, harmonious mixture of Western and Eastern styles.

Kamala and Masha ate their delayed breakfast with ravenous hunger, but Jana had little appetite. The old woman had been with Omar for over an hour. Jana had left her to do whatever mumbo-jumbo she was going to do, because after what Omar had said, she couldn't stop the proceedings, but neither could she bear to watch.

She was crushingly aware that whatever his injuries, they were her fault. If she had not reacted so impulsively, if she had investigated only a little before setting off on that trip across the unknown…in retrospect she could hardly believe her own actions. To take two princesses, their father's only heirs, alone on such a trip, knowing nothing of the way and little of the destination!

She must have been crazy. And if Prince Omar died as a result of her actions…if his wounds festered…if his skull was fractured in spite of what the old woman had said…if his condition deteriorated without any way of getting help…everything could be laid at Jana's door. She and she alone was responsible. Several times she made up her mind to take the Land Rover back to the palace, and every time she decided that the attempt would be useless and she was needed here. Finally she made up her mind that if Omar was worse rather than better tonight, she would leave at midnight to make her way to the nearest phone, and then, if she could successfully elude Jalal and his men, return.

When Doktar Amina had gone, with smiles and reassurances to the princesses, Jana asked Baba Musa, through Masha, first, where the nearest phone would be. Baba Musa had no idea, so she asked who could be hired to take a letter to the palace.

They were all in the kitchen. Baba Musa was breaking up bits of firewood and laying them inside the ancient black cast iron cookstove that dominated one corner of the big room. He agreed that this might be possible if Prince Omar wished it, lit his fire and closed the little iron door. He genially suggested that Jana should cook something for Prince Omar to eat, as he was sure to be hungry.

She stared at Masha, who had interpreted, and then at Baba Musa. "Is he awake?" she demanded.

"Oh, yes, Jana Khanum," Masha replied. "Doktar Amina said so."

She tore out of the kitchen, but managed to slow to a more sedate pace before she got to Omar's room. The door was open and she went in.

Omar was awake and lying propped up in the bed, his

head and leg expertly bandaged. His eyes seemed clearer. She could smell the lingering odor of the black muck.

"How are you?" she asked softly.

Omar grunted. "Well enough." He closed his eyes, and she quelled the desperate apology that was on her lips. The last thing he needed was strong emotion. She could apologize another day.

"I'm going to make you something to eat," she said. "Do you think you could eat some soup?"

He opened his eyes. "This is not your job, to wait on me like a servant!"

An hour ago he had been calling her *Janam*. She supposed that meant that, whatever Doktar Amina had done, he was improved. Her cheeks grew hot. "It wasn't my job to get you wounded, either!" she said tartly. "So suppose we call it even?"

He grinned, his teeth looking very white against the neat black beard, and she took this for agreement and went out again.

"Excellent!" said Omar a few minutes later. He had propped himself more upright in the bed, but still looked grey and haggard.

"I've put the soup in a cup," she said, pulled the chair close by the bed and sat, balancing the tray on her lap. She spread a small towel over the blanket in front of him, then handed him a spoon and the big mug of soup. On the tray were salt and pepper and some hot *naan*.

He was too ill and too hungry to protest at this invalid treatment. He ate in silence for a few minutes. "Very good," he murmured, and took the offered bread.

"Omar," she said, "I think we should send a message to the palace. I've asked Baba Musa to find someone willing to make the trip, but he would like you to instruct him personally."

"You are right," said Omar. He finished the soup and

set the cup on the tray. "We will send a message tonight after sunset."

"Shall I tell Baba Musa you want him to find someone?" Jana asked, relieved.

Omar shook his head. "There will be no one in the village to go, except by mule, and that will take many days," he said. "There is another way."

Fatigue assailed him suddenly, and he closed his eyes. Worried as she was, Jana knew she could not press him for details now. Praying that he would still be conscious enough later to tell her how to send the message, she picked up the tray, softly went out and closed the door.

The princesses at least were confident that their father was going to recover after Doktar Amina's ministrations, and were restored to all their delight in being where they were. They went gaily off down the valley with Baba Musa and returned with sackloads of fresh vegetables, lamb, herbs, cheese, yogurt, olives, flour, fresh goats' milk and olive oil. There was no refrigerator in the house—there was no electricity—but Baba Musa took her underneath the house, part of which was on stilts, lifted a wooden door in the ground and showed her a deep hole. He pulled on a rope and a metal basket came up.

"*Yak,*" he said, smiling and pointing down into the hole. Jana leaned over and saw huge lumps of ice piled at the bottom. No doubt they had been tossed down there last winter, and would last till the first snowfall.

"*Yak?*" she repeated. She wrapped her arms around herself and mimed shivering cold.

"*Baleh, baleh!*" cried Baba Musa, nodding and smiling. Jana loaded the perishable supplies into the basket and watched them disappear into the hole. It suddenly dawned on her just how primitive a place they had come to. She prayed that Omar had not been dreaming when he spoke of sending a message. The sooner they got him back to civilisation, the better.

* * *

"You should not be required to cook," Omar said, when she presented him with another meal that afternoon. He had slept and looked much better. The grey pallor was gone. He did not want invalid foods, and she had made him a sandwich of thinly sliced lamb steak, which he devoured ravenously.

Jana merely smiled. "That's all right. I had the girls helping me."

"That is good." He nodded. "What girls?"

She laughed. "Masha and Kamala," she informed him. "Your daughters."

He turned and directed a searching gaze on her. "The princesses are not kitchen help."

"No, I know they aren't!" Jana said gaily. "They don't know one end of a frying pan from the other! But they are very willing, and quick learners. Kamala crumbled the goat's cheese for your salad."

"Miss Stewart." Prince Omar laid down his fork. "Masha will be queen of this country one day."

She frowned in amazement. "So what? So they shouldn't learn how to cope with the basic necessities of life?"

"It is not appropriate to—"

"Appropriate?" She had met this attitude before. It was exactly a match for her father's, and she hated it.

"They are—"

"Any life skill is appropriate to anyone," she interrupted ruthlessly. "Excuse me, but not so long ago you told me my job was seeing that they escaped from what you call the petty rivalries of the harem!"

"And how will breaking up goat's cheese help them do that?"

She flushed at the tone. "It will make them self-sufficient!" She struggled to keep her temper. She was sure he should not be agitated. "Do you really believe that a woman who can read foreign language newspapers but can't lift a finger to take care of her own physical needs is going to be a fitting queen for the hardworking people of this country? What will Masha and Kamala have in common with them?''

''Nothing. Why should they?''

''*You* fly a helicopter!''

''Of course I do. I served in the military for two years, according to my father's wish.''

''I rest my case!'' Then almost immediately, she said remorsefully, ''I'm sorry, I shouldn't be arguing with you in your condition. But really, you'll just have to accept it. There is no one to do the work except ourselves.''

''It is of no consequence,'' he said, with regal stiffness. So he was definitely improved in health.

''Anyway,'' said Jana, unable to resist getting in the last word, ''in the kitchen they're improving their English by leaps and bounds, and you must approve of that!''

Prince Omar made no reply. But she could see that he did not think words like *frying pan* were a significant gain to the princesses' vocabulary.

At eight o'clock that night, following his instructions, she returned to Omar's bedroom. Omar was sitting on the side of the bed, trying to stand on his good leg. Jana rushed to his side, and felt him lean on her.

''It's too soon to try walking!'' she reproached him.

He knew she was right, and lay down again without protest.

When he was comfortable, Jana took a deep breath. ''Prince Omar, I've got to say this now, or I'll lose the courage to do it,'' she began.

He raised his eyebrows. He could still look forbidding in spite of his wounds, and Jana suddenly felt how much she feared the expression of his displeasure.

But she had to face it.

''It was so stupid!'' she cried. ''People say I'm impulsive, but this was really—I can hardly believe myself I did this!''

''You did not expect such consequences, I think,'' he said mildly. Startled, both by his reaction and the force of her relief, she blinked at him for a moment.

''*Of course* I didn't, but to embark on something so extreme when I was totally ignorant of the dangers is just... I'm sorry, please believe I'm desperately sorry. I—''

She broke off because he lifted his hand. She was suddenly aware how weak he must feel. He did not need strong emotions.

''What is done is done,'' he said.

Jana heaved a sigh. ''Thank you.''

''Now we must act.'' He paused, breathing.

She realized suddenly that he had been on his feet for a purpose.

''What do you want?'' she asked.

Omar nodded towards a large wood relief carving on the wall. ''Please lift that down,'' he said.

Behind the carving was the door of a safe. Omar handed her a key and dictated a sequence of numbers, and mystified, half-expecting to find a radio set, she pulled open the heavy door.

There was no radio set inside, though there might have been room for one. There were several boxes of various sizes and shapes, wood and metal.

''There is a metal box on the left. Please bring that.''

She found it and placed it on the bed beside him. It was unlocked. Omar opened it to reveal several sticks of what looked, to Jana's inexperienced eyes, like dynamite, in a box that had once held eighteen or a dozen.

Omar gazed at the contents for a moment of surprise. ''Three left,'' he murmured. He glanced into Jana's curious face, then back at the box. He stroked his beard with one thoughtful finger, then removed all three. Jana replaced the empty box in the safe and locked it again.

"Flares?" she guessed.

"Ashraf Durran will be watching now."

It was the first time she had breathed easy since the moment when she heard the helicopter go down. Under instructions from Omar, Jana carried the flares onto the balcony to fire them off. She ignited the first and then stood back as, with a choking sound and a bang, it took off. A long red bullet sailed skywards for several long seconds and then went off like an exploding lightbulb. Suddenly the night around them was as bright as day.

Jana blinked, trying to get her night vision back, and then ignited the second flare. It too went off, throwing a powerful light over the whole horizon.

But when she lit the third, either it was defective, or she had jolted it out of position, for instead of flying up, it leapt convulsively over the railing and nosedived to the earth a few yards below. Jana blinked down at it, watching helplessly as it shot violent sparks into the earth for a few minutes and then died.

She returned to Omar's bedroom. He was watching her gravely. "What happened?"

"I don't really know. It just went down instead of up," she said.

"It is of no consequence," said Prince Omar.

"I hope Ashraf Durran was watching," Jana said worriedly. "Do you think he was?"

"Yes, I think he was," said Prince Omar, in a curiously detached voice. He was looking into the distance, a slight frown drawing his thickly marked eyebrows together.

"You think he saw the two I set off?"

"Yes, he saw them."

The little girls were delighted with their summer wardrobes. Shorts and T-shirts gave them a freedom they had not experienced before, and Jana watched them running and playing in the summer sun with a carefree joy she had never seen in them at the palace, not even in the pool.

She explained to Baba Musa what she wanted, and he went away and came back with two empty oil drums and some logs and built a raft, and Jana continued with swimming and diving lessons. The water in the lake was crystal clear, spring fed, very deep. It seemed to have a magic about it. The princesses loved swimming in the lake, and so did Jana, and their laughter rang out over the water and echoed from the surrounding hills.

Prince Omar did not approve. After a few days he was well enough to be helped out to the balcony by Baba Musa, and would sit for a while. Sometimes in such moments, she looked up at the balcony of the house and saw Omar there, watching with a face like stone. She wondered what it was about their unfettered joy that made him look so angry.

Summoned by Baba Musa, a woman came from a village further down the valley to do the cooking, but when she saw that Jana was able-bodied, she grew puzzled. She was very willing to serve her prince. But she clearly did not grasp the concept of "servant." That one person should work at two jobs in order to minister to the needs of another, while that other did nothing, or only supervised children, was beyond her.

Jana had no intention of disillusioning such a deep-dyed democratic spirit. Through her faithful interpreters, who were growing more adept by the hour, she asked the woman to teach her to bake *naan*. This the woman could comprehend. For two days the four females scarcely left the kitchen, except to take Omar his meals, while Rudaba tutored them in her arts.

When the two days were over, Jana and the princesses had had a crash course in Middle Eastern cooking. They had several oven-ready casseroles and cooked dishes on ice at the bottom of the cooler, and Jana had a dozen scribbled recipes, half of them calling for ingredients whose name she only knew in Parvani.

Then, with smiles and nods, and waving vigorously, Rudaba went home.

Jana had expected the arrival of a helicopter the morning after she sent off the emergency flares. When it did not happen she thought the rescue must be coming by land. But when day followed day and there was no appearance, she began to forget about it. There was, in fact, no emergency. Whatever Doktar Amina was doing, and the wise woman came regularly to visit her patient, Omar was progressing day by day.

On the morning he hobbled downstairs for the first time, using a rough-made staff Baba Musa had made him, he found Jana, Masha and Kamala in the large kitchen making breakfast. Masha was on a low stool, by the stove, with one of the iron plates off, holding bread on a long fork over the flames to make toast. Kamala was carefully counting out three sets of cutlery onto one tray, and one set onto another. Jana was breaking eggs into a bowl.

They did not hear his approach because they were singing.

"'There are snakes, ants that sting, and other creeping things, in an English country ga-arden,'" they sang, and then, as he entered, Masha whirled and cried out, clapping a startled hand to her chest.

"*Baba!* You are walking! Oh, look, you made me drop the bread into the fire!" she admonished him, in a tone he had never heard on his daughters' lips before.

Jana paused wordlessly, an egg in her hand, and Kamala smiled at him, her hands full of knives and forks. "Good morning, Baba," the latter said happily.

"Good morning," said Omar. "You are all very busy."

"We are making breakfast, Baba," Kamala informed him unnecessarily.

"So I see."

He did not often converse with his daughters in English; it was a new and slightly disorienting experience for him.

"Good morning," said Jana. "Will you eat with us? We eat on the verandah."

"Yes, thank you," said Omar.

Jana calmly turned to Kamala, impervious to Omar's disapproving frown. "You can put all four place settings onto the one tray, then, Kamala. You don't need the other one anymore."

"Yes, Jana Khanum."

Jana pulled out a chair beside the big wooden table, and Omar hobbled to it and sat. "Where is Rudaba this morning? Not here yet?" he asked.

Masha put another piece of slightly charred toast onto the plate and turned. "Rudaba has a new granddaughter, Baba!" she exclaimed. "She doesn't come anymore."

Omar frowned. "Who has been cooking all the meals?"

"*We* have, Baba! Jana Khanum and Kamala and me! It was a big secret!" She giggled. "And every time, you say it is delicious, don't you?"

Omar stared levelly at Jana. "Yes," he agreed softly. "Every time, I say it is delicious."

"Have you got everything on the tray, Kamala?" asked Jana. "Then I'll take it out onto the verandah and you can lay the table."

Trailed by a skipping Kamala, she suited the action to the words. When she returned to the kitchen, Masha chirruped, "I have made all the toast, Jana Khanum! Now may I stir the eggs?"

So under Omar's piercing gaze, Jana placed the black cast iron pan over the flames and held the bowl of goat's butter while Masha dug out a spoonful and tossed it in. Together they poured the eggs into the pan, and Masha stood over it with a wooden spatula in her hand, carefully stirring.

When Kamala came back into the kitchen with the empty tray, she exclaimed, "We forgot to get the milk from the cooler, Jana Khanum!"

"We'll do it now," said Jana, and the two went out.

Omar watched the proceedings in silence until, a few minutes later, he was invited out to the verandah to settle himself at the table there. It was a beautiful morning, and Jana's heart was suddenly singing. On the hillside on the opposite side of the lake a small herd of goats moved up the slope, their bells ringing and their cries carrying on the pure, clear air. Behind them, in the distance, the rugged, massive peak of Mount Shir presided over the scene.

Jana looked from the white-topped mountain to the face of Prince Omar and thought that he was like the mountain—tall, cold, remote. As far as she knew, none of the mountains in these ranges had ever been volcanic. Was Omar, she wondered? Or was he as cold at the center as he seemed on the surface? He seemed miles away now from the man who, not long ago, had called her *Janam* and *Mashouka*.

The princesses were slightly subdued in his presence, their high spirits toned down. When she asked them if Baba Musa was coming over this morning to take them fishing, they nodded vigorously but did not burst into the chattering excitement they would usually have shown.

She saw Omar blink. "Do you go fishing with Baba Musa?" he asked them.

"Yes, Baba, he is teaching us to catch fish! On Tuesday I caught one on my own fishing pole! And we ate it for lunch!"

Over the head of his happily chattering daughter, Omar's green gaze, so dark it was nearly black, was pinning Jana to her chair.

"Have you finished, children? Then run down to the lake. I am going to chat with Jana Khanum."

Jana took a deep breath and shook her head. "Dishes

first!'' she carolled, and without protest Masha and Kamala ran to bring the tray and help her load it.

Keeping his temper with some effort, Omar asked, ''Who does the dishes?''

''We all do, Baba!'' Kamala told him confidingly. ''Jana Khanum says when everyone helps, the work is easy. I like to wash best, because the water is warm and there are suds!''

When the tray was full, Jana picked it up and, flashing a slightly challenging glance at Omar, carried it into the kitchen, accompanied by her two able helpers. After a moment Omar struggled to his feet and followed.

It had taken Jana two days to figure out that the water in one of the compartments of the stove wasn't a functional part of the stove system, but a reservoir method of heating water for use. Now she held the washbowl while Masha carefully ladled out the warm water into it, and carried it to the table.

''If you will permit me,'' Omar said, ''I will do Masha and Kamala's share of the washing.''

Jana knew she couldn't put off the showdown any longer. She shrugged and waited as the princesses thanked their father and ran out.

Ten

"**D**o you want an apron?" she offered, moving towards the washbowl as he limped in behind her. He had left his stick on the verandah.

"A what?"

She was tying one around her own waist, and she held up the one that Masha usually wore. They were all makeshift; she had stitched ties on the edges of dish towels. "Apron. You never heard the word?"

"In English?" he demanded irritably. "No. Who would say this word to me?"

"Well, you learn something every day!"

"Yes, indeed I learned something today!" Omar took the apron from her outstretched hand and tossed it onto the table. He moved closer to her, and Jana involuntarily stepped back. He was in a towering rage, and Omar in a rage was pretty overwhelming. "I learn that you are making my daughters into household servants! I had told you this was not my will! In the palace they are forbidden even to go into the kitchens! Yet you persisted! Why is this?''

Her skin was prickling with nerves, but after that one false step she was determined to hold her ground. ''Somebody has to do the work, Omar,'' she told him. ''Who exactly in this household do you imagine is the appropriate person to do the work?''

''*No one* in this household! That is why Rudaba came! You have sent her away!''

She gazed levelly at him, determined not to be cowed by his anger. ''Who did the work last time you were here with the princesses, Your Highness?''

He was a little taken aback. ''Naturally, I brought staff with me from the palace.''

''Well, this time you didn't! And if you have the colossal arrogance to ask a woman who already has a full day's work to do running her own family to come and run yours in addition, rather than let your daughters engage in a little physical labor, then you're not a king, you're a despot!''

He felt exasperated with her. He had never felt so angry or thwarted by a woman in his life. ''Village women need money as well as those in the city! The Bahrami tribe is sworn to help the house of Durran! She was not unwilling when Baba Musa spoke to her!''

He was shouting, and Jana was now losing the battle to maintain her own relative calm. ''Of course she was not unwilling! You're the king and you've been hurt! But when she saw me she naturally assumed I would do the work, and wanted to go home to her new granddaughter.''

''There must be another woman—'' he began.

''Do you really think it is right for a prince to think that he only has to snap his fingers and any of his subjects should abandon their lives to become his slave? You're not just arrogant, you're an anachronism! They have even less here than in the city, you know! All the water has to be carried from wells, or the river! It's backbreaking work!''

The injustice of this infuriated him further. "I know this!" he shouted. "That is why I asked Rudaba to come! Because this work is too hard and too much for you!"

But she overrode that. "In addition, as it happens, Rudaba looks after the goats and her sick daughter and the new baby, and grows her own vegetables! Probably all the women are much the same! Truthfully, Omar, how do you think your needs stack up against that?"

"It is not fitting that the princesses should engage in menial tasks!"

"Well, if that's an invitation to me to do all the work, forget it! I'm no slave either! We all eat, and in my opinion it will do Masha and Kamala no harm whatsoever to learn how much work is involved in the business of providing for their physical needs. It should teach them genuine respect and compassion for their servants in future."

His eyes narrowed dangerously. "They will learn compassion and respect for their servants and subjects without this, Jana! I teach it to them," he growled, using her first name for the first time without seeming to notice. "You too are a descendant of kings! It is not fitting that you are hauling water and lighting fires like a…like a…"

The fact that he couldn't find the words enraged him still further. But he was cut off anyway.

"Don't tell me what's *fitting!*" she shouted furiously. "My *mother* didn't think it was fitting that I come to work for *you,* come to that, and if I listened to everybody's opinion of what was *fitting* for me, I'd be at home married to the most boring man I ever met! Now, if you don't mind, *I* consider it *perfectly* fitting, under the circumstances, to do the dishes, and the water's getting cold!"

She turned to the washing bowl, dropped in a few soapflakes and furiously swished the water. Omar's eyes widened, then narrowed. He was not used to being contradicted so loudly, or dismissed with such high-handedness.

He put his hand on her shoulder and turned her to face

him. "I—" he began, but Jana held up a drying cloth. He stiffened.

"What is this?" he demanded.

"Well, it has several names in English, depending on the region. Dish towel and tea towel are the most common," she returned. He glared at her and she glared right back. "I hope you haven't forgotten you're doing Masha and Kamala's share. Or did you imagine that I would take up the slack for—?"

His eyes grew blacker and blacker through this speech. He lifted his hand and she flinched and fell silent, the words choked in her throat, as he tore the dish towel from her hand and flung it aside. Then his strong fingers gripped her upper arms.

"Have you finished?" he asked. And slowly, as they stared into each other's eyes and her lips parted on a soundless gasp, everything changed. Her fury metamorphosed and became a rage of a different kind. She felt heat spreading out from under his hands into her heart and stomach and breasts. Two flames, but not of anger, ignited in his dark eyes. Jana felt her body coming closer to his, but whether he drew her, or she moved, or whether some impersonal magnetic field drew them both, she did not know.

"*Janam,*" he whispered. *My soul.* The word ignited a spark in her that had been burning unseen since the day she had brought him here, bloody and half-dead.

"Omar," she moaned, and at the look in his eyes now she trembled. It was passionate, all-consuming, a firestorm of need.

Then her body was pressed to his, his arms were around her, and with convulsive hunger and need, his mouth found hers. Sensation swam meltingly along her limbs, sparks shot and sang through her blood, and her mouth responded with equal need to the questing of his lips. His hand encircled her throat and lifted her chin higher to his hungry kiss.

"Baba! Baba!" The high cry was accompanied by the sound of footsteps on the wooden floor of the verandah, and they broke apart and turned towards the door.

Masha burst in. "Baba Musa is here, Baba! Please will you come fishing with us?"

He carefully stepped away from Jana. "My leg will not let me get into the boat yet, Masha," he explained gently, and with a few words the child ran out again. A moment later they heard her cry *"Baba naymiayad!"* Daddy is not coming.

Jana heaved a deep breath, and looked anywhere but at Omar. Then she heard his voice, controlled and distant, as she had heard it many times before.

"I am sorry, Miss Stewart. It will not happen again."

She gasped and looked at him. "Omar—"

Omar lifted a hand, and the words died on her lips. But he only reached to take the towel from the table.

She couldn't tear her gaze from him. He turned his head and the dark green look took nothing, gave nothing. "Let us do the dishes," said Prince Omar.

He was no stranger to sexual desire for a woman. He was not used to it coming over him so unexpectedly, nor feeling that he was not in control. He did not like it. He believed that the feelings that had overcome him with Jana were the result of a period of abstinence, no more, but for all the reasons that he had resisted his sexual interest in her from the beginning, he must resist now, he told himself. He would not use the situation to take sexual advantage of her. He would be more careful in future.

He did not allow himself to feel that it was more than abstinence that fuelled his passion, or fear that underlay his decision to deny it. He did not admit to himself that something more than sexual desire drew him to his daughters' English tutor.

But under siege on the battlefield he had never more

fervently wished for reinforcements than he now wished for the arrival of Ashraf Durran.

Jana, too, now found the prolonged stay becoming intolerable. She found it more and more difficult to be in Omar's company. Something had come awake in her with Omar's kiss, and she wanted more. She yearned for him, for his touch, to see that flame in his eyes again. To have him call her *my soul* in that hoarse, hungry voice.

But it was very clear that Omar intended it should never happen again.

As Omar's injuries healed, Jana discovered that, whatever he felt was appropriate for the princesses, he was quite capable of taking care of his own physical needs. He was a sort of craftsman, able to mend nearly anything, a skill he said he had learned in the navy, and he could cook, and from that first day when he came downstairs, the four of them did the dishes together every night.

That was the time when she taught the princesses songs in English. They loved it, and she saw no reason to change things when Prince Omar joined them. At first he did not join in, but the easygoing atmosphere that Jana had created had changed the princesses' ideas. They were as adaptable as any children, and although they still exhibited great respect for their father, they had unconsciously become less frightened of him.

"Why don't you sing, Baba?" Kamala demanded at last. "It would be more fun if you sang, too!"

This was not an argument anyone had ever put to Prince Omar Durran ibn Daud ibn Hassan al Quraishi. "More fun?" he repeated with a blink.

"When you don't sing it's not so nice." Masha gravely came to her sister's support. "Don't you like singing, Baba?"

He was on the ropes. Never before in his life had he felt

at a disadvantage with his own children, but of course he had rarely before this come into such constant contact with them. Certainly he had never done domestic chores with them.

"I don't know the words," Omar protested, with the feebleness of the challenged male anywhere in the world.

"But we will teach you, just the way Jana Khanum taught us!" carolled Masha, glad to discover the root of the problem. In a high, sweet voice she suddenly sang the refrain of a Beatles song. "La la la la…"

To his own surprise, he found himself laughing. "What do these words mean—obladi, oblada?"

"Nothing, Baba!" Masha cried, in high delight. "Mo—Jana Khanum says they are just sounds!"

He flicked a glance to Jana over his daughters' heads, and they exchanged the kind of look that was both balm and torment to her. "This is to teach them English?" he chided, amused.

"Western culture, too," she said. Then she turned to the girls. "Shall we teach Baba a whole song? A song we know all the words to?"

"Yes!" cried Masha and Kamala together. "You would like that, wouldn't you, Baba?" Masha asked.

Omar was drying a bowl with a certain piratical flair. He looked down at his daughter. She was gazing up at him with complete trust and adoration. "Yes," he said, because he suddenly found himself reluctant to dash her spirits. "Yes, I would like to learn a song you all know."

As though the valley had its own compelling time, Jana had begun to wake every morning when the first rays of the sun struck the lake, and her day started then. Like the village women farther along the valley, Jana had a lot of work to get through in a day. The house lacked any modern convenience.

Although there was a small reservoir on the side of the

stove, most of their hot water came from an oil drum set up on a grid over a fire outdoors. When needed, that fire had to be lit, and the drum filled, bucketful by bucketful, from the well. Hot water for washing clothes or for baths was carried from the drum to the tub by the bucketful and everything was washed and scrubbed by hand.

There was, fortunately, plenty of soap in the house, but none of it was detergent-based, and Jana gained a new appreciation of the difference between *dirt* and *stain* and a more tolerant understanding of the stained garments that all the villagers, including Doktar Amina, wore. Many stains were impossible to get out of the princesses' white shorts even when she adopted the advanced technology she had observed by the river near the city—spreading the wet clothes on a large rock and beating the stain with a smooth stone.

It was while she was putting away some of Omar's clothes in his bedroom that she made the discovery that he had an extensive wardrobe of casual clothes, many of them Western jeans, shirts and T-shirts.

"I'd like to commandeer some of your clothes," she told him that evening, after the children were in bed. Although Baba Musa always went home just before dark, and most of the villagers seemed to go to bed with the sun as well as get up with it, Jana could never sleep without a couple of hours of relative relaxation at the end of the day.

Omar joined her. Sometimes they sat in the sitting room and read or worked by lamplight and even—occasionally, on those evenings when the mountain chill came right down into the valley—by the light from a fire in the curiously made fireplace.

"Commandeer?" he repeated. He liked it when she used words he did not know, and Jana had to be always ready to define any word she used so that he could add it to his vocabulary. It wasn't always easy.

She grinned and shook her head, feeling a little caught

out. "Well, I think it means when the army seizes something—like a private ship, for example—to use in war."

He flicked her a glance. "What war will my clothes be needed for?"

"The war against nakedness in the rest of us," Jana replied, laughing. "I've found a few clothes the girls left here from before, but Kamala's are all too small. A few of Masha's now fit Kamala, but Masha and I have very little in our wardrobes."

She held up the torn shorts she was attempting to mend with a piece cut from one of Kamala's too-small garments.

"The girls can wear your T-shirts as dresses, and with a belt I could probably wear your pants—and a few more shirts will be a real blessing."

"Share them out as suits you, Jana," he said. He was aware that the thought gave him pleasure.

Fish were plentiful in the lake, which was just as well, because Baba Musa's techniques for catching them were not far removed from the bent-pin-on-a-string method. One day Jana decided to go along on the fishing expedition.

"Why?" said Omar, frowning.

"Because if anything happened to Baba Musa, we would want to be self-sufficient," she explained patiently. "I haven't been fishing since I was Kamala's age, and I think it's something I—everyone!—should know how to do." He was sitting on the ground beside her as she grubbed for worms and other morsels with which to tempt the fish, with a pleasure both immediate and nostalgic. She hadn't done this since those long-ago, carefree summer holidays on her uncle's estate, before her parents' breakup. "After all, I eat the fish, why shouldn't I know how to catch them?"

Jana was in blue jean cutoffs, bare feet, and one of his shirts with the tails tied around her waist. Her long limbs were warmly tanned after so many days in the sun. He watched her intent digging with deep pleasure. One strand of hair kept escaping from the knot she had secured it in on the top of her head, and one earth-covered hand kept futilely pushing it up out of her way. "On this reasoning, you should ask Baba Musa to teach you how to slaughter a goat," he pointed out mildly.

"Well, and if we're going to be here much longer, I'll do that," Jana said. "Anyway, he says it's easy. You just slit the throat as it's lying in the field and it falls asleep as it loses blood and never knows."

Omar laughed. Even though he now almost expected to be constantly surprised by her, still she managed to surprise him. "You have asked Baba Musa the details of how to slaughter a goat?" he demanded in disbelief.

"Why not? You may not have noticed, but we've been eating goat's meat."

He smiled quizzically at her, so that her heart pounded, and Jana resolutely quelled her quick response. "Of course I know it. It is a national dish. Which of my daughters translated the gruesome details for you?"

She smiled smugly. "Neither. I'm picking up some Parvani, you know! But anyway, he did it mostly with sign language." She mimicked Baba Musa miming first the goat and then the human, the goat sitting comfortably in the field, the human coming up and stroking it, a little knife hidden in his hand, the lifted chin, quick, gentle cut, and then the goat again, blinking, and slowly, dreamily falling asleep.

Omar erupted into laughter—hearty, healthy laughter of a kind he hadn't felt in himself for years. "You are too pretty a goat. If you blinked like that at the goatherd you would live to a very old age," he told her, and unconsciously reached out to push the errant strand of hair back for her.

Jana froze, her breath stopped in her throat, and waited for his touch. In the same moment he awoke to his own unconscious action. He drew his hand away.

"Well, anyway," Jana said brusquely, dusting off her bare legs and standing up, "that's for another day! Today is fishing!" She held up the small tin of worms and grubs she had collected, and smiled at him, but it was a formal smile: the confiding manner of a moment ago was gone.

He was aware of a stab of regret. But it could not be otherwise.

Omar was sitting on his balcony when the fishing expedition returned to shore. He had heard their shouts of triumph and disaster during the course of the afternoon, across the water, and now Jana, Masha and Kamala scrambled out and stood holding up their catches for his admiration and approval.

"Baba, Baba, I caught another fish!"

They were all wet, grubby, and happy as the goats on the far side of the hill. He stood up and came to the railing. "How many did you get?"

Masha appointed herself spokesman. "Baba Musa got four, and Kamala got one and I got two!"

"And how many did Jana Khanum get?"

"None, Baba! She said it was very furst—furst—frurstating, Baba! Everybody caught one but Jana Khanum!"

"Poor Jana Khanum," he teased, and smiled down at them. He had never seen his daughters so dirty, he reflected. But then, he had never seen them so carefree and happy, either. He had almost forgotten that such a state could exist. He had been so determined to give his daughters the education his mother and his wife had never had—had he forgotten other needs that were just as important? Or had he simply been dismissing happiness as not possible to those who must rule?

He had not been happy since the day he married, twelve years ago. He had accepted the marriage as his duty then—his mother had told him it was his duty and he had believed her. When it proved to be a deeply unhappy union both for him and his wife, he had accepted that that was the price of being born to rule.

No doubt he had carried that attitude over to his daughters' upbringing. But standing here, looking at two happy, excited, exhausted children, he could not believe that they would make less able rulers because they had experienced such simple pleasures. How could he believe it? It was ridiculous. Yet somewhere in his heart he had believed it, until this moment.

Those who rule have no right to think of happiness.

Something in him seemed to crack and break, and fall away. It was one of the bands around his heart.

When he had made his awkward way downstairs, Baba Musa had gone home, and Jana was struggling with the cleaning of the fish while the two princesses watched interestedly over her shoulder. Her knife was not quite sharp enough, and she had blood and guts smeared over her hands and arms, and even on her cheek.

"Why did not Baba Musa do this for you?" Omar asked mildly.

"Because I told him it wasn't necessary!"

"Is this another one of those things everyone should be able to do?"

"Yes, it is!" Jana snapped. Truth to tell, she would rather have learned it another day, but she knew Baba Musa was eager to get home. She was tired out and would have loved to just be able to cook the fish. And Baba Musa was an expert. She had watched him clean fish on other days and it took him about five seconds per fish. It was taking her several minutes.

"Shall I do it for you?" Omar inquired mildly.

She glared up at him. "This from the man who disapproves of fishing? Do you know how?"

He shrugged. "Men have a knack for such things. It is not so distasteful to us."

Jana merely rolled her eyes at him and went on with her task.

"There are four fish here," Omar observed next. "One is Kamala's, and two are Masha's. Who caught the fourth fish?"

Jana ignored him. Masha said, "Baba Musa gave us one of his, Baba! So that we could have one each for supper."

"That was very kind of Baba Musa," Omar said. "Of course you thanked him."

"Yes, Baba," the two princesses chorused.

"Did you catch a fish for me, Masha?"

He was surprised by the adoring glance that his daughter threw up at him. "Yes, Baba," she said with a shy smile.

"It will be delicious," he said. He touched her cheek, and her eyes glowed.

"I like to catch fish for you, Baba," she said.

"Poor Jana Khanum!" he said, as they turned back to where she still struggled. "She did not catch a fish for herself. It is a good thing Baba Musa was so generous!"

"Damn it to hell!" Jana cried, as the dull knife slipped and stabbed her hand.

"This has certainly been educational for all concerned," Omar observed. "I suppose you feel that everyone should be able to swear in several languages, Jana Khanum?"

He could not remember ever having teased a woman before. He watched his two daughters laughing and Jana's reluctant grin, and felt the stirrings of a freedom he didn't know existed.

Eleven

Two days later, Jana was awakened by a tapping at her balcony window. It was Omar. Filled with a sudden alarm, she flung herself off the bed and rushed to open the door.

He was dressed in worn jeans and a T-shirt and looked perfectly healthy. "Omar!" Jana whispered hoarsely, her system still pumping adrenaline. "What's the matter?" Behind him, the world was still grey with the dawn shadow of the mountains. "What time is it?"

"Five-thirty. Nothing is wrong. Will you get dressed and come with me? I have something to show you."

This reminded her that she was standing there in little more than a T-shirt. She was more covered than when she went swimming, but somehow the proximity of the bed made her feel very naked. "All right," she said. "Five minutes?"

"You will need shoes," Omar advised, and she closed the door, then dressed in record time. When she came down the stairs he was in the kitchen slinging a small knapsack over his shoulder. He nodded briskly and led her outside.

The path he chose led to the river. She had explored that far, but on reaching the river he turned and followed it uphill, where she had never been. The path was rocky and a bit difficult, and Omar's leg, she was sure, was still far from fully healed, but although they went slowly over rougher terrain, he showed no signs of discomfort in the climb.

Worried, she said nothing. It was going to be another beautiful day, and the sun was just now cresting the peaks of the distant mountains to pour its golden lava on the valley and the lake behind and below them.

After about twenty minutes, they reached a pretty, sheltered spot, where a few trees overhung a widening of the river, and it formed a kind of pool. Here Omar stopped, swung the knapsack off his shoulder and tossed it lightly to the ground. Then he bent over, lifted a tarpaulin, and she noticed a green metal box on the ground near a large rock...and a long fishing rod case leaning against it.

She stared at it uncomprehendingly for a moment. Then she understood the significance of what she was seeing. "Omar!" she cried indignantly.

"You had such a bad day's fishing that day that I thought it would please you to have a chance with some proper equipment," he said.

"Omar!" she cried again.

"Quiet, don't scare the fish. This is a very good spot early in the morning," he went on calmly. "You are sure to catch something here. Shall I teach you how to cast?"

And with that he picked up a rod and moved to the riverbank. Her jaw still open with outraged surprise, Jana followed him.

"The trout in this river are delicious," Omar told her as he fastened a shimmering turquoise-and-green fly to his line, the corners of his mouth not even twitching.

"Omar, you—you—how could you *do* that to me?" Jana demanded, beginning to laugh.

He flicked her a glance of amused tenderness that she would cherish all the rest of her days. "Do? I? What did I do?"

"Don't you play innocent with me!" Jana commanded in dire tones. "You know perfectly well you—and you let me clean those fish, too! I suppose you're an expert at it!"

"But it was an educational experience! I offered to clean the fish for you. You refused," he pointed out mildly over his shoulder as he straightened and prepared to cast. "I offer you another kind of fishing education this morning. Watch."

Although he was managing to control his physical desire for her, Omar had not yet noticed that the pleasure he took in her company was equally a danger. Nor did he notice how much he was changing. The first few times he had laughed and teased her had seemed strange to him. But laughter had been natural to him as a youth, and he was gaining back parts of his old self without noticing it. At the palace, he might have been more on guard. But here, the scene of so much childhood happiness, his subtly growing joy seemed natural.

Jana of course could not resist the pleasures offered. Being with Omar was both the deepest pleasure and the hardest pain she had ever experienced. Nothing had prepared her for what it meant to be so deeply attracted to a man who did not return the feeling. She soared and swooped between joy and heartbreak, and gratefully treasured the crumbs that fell her way.

She could not have refused to let him teach her fly fishing, though she knew in her heart she was storing up misery with such moments as these.

He flicked his wrist, and sent the line neatly into the little swirl of eddies that formed at the head of the natural pool, where the fly delicately lit on the water and then sank.

"Notice that I cast at the head of the pool and let the river carry the fly down into the still water," he said. "The fish feed in the pool."

She watched obediently as the line was carried into the pool and then further down. When it had reached another place where the water began rushing over rocks, he pulled his line in again.

"Would you like to try a cast?" Omar asked, offering her the rod.

Jana took the rod and approached the bank. He stood close, and only then, when heat pervaded his body, began to realize how his morning's impulse had betrayed him. "Now, hold it behind you," he advised, stepping away from her. "You make a short jab forward, not very far, let the line travel," he said.

She learned quickly. He saw that she had a natural physical intelligence, and his thoughts swiftly jumped. He wondered who had first taught her sex and whether she had been so quick to respond to that tuition. He watched the fly lift from the water and sink in again, watched her slim wrist gain in confidence in the cast, watched her smile of triumph as the fish came to her, time and again, as if she had only to request their sacrifice and they leapt to make it.

He looked at the long brown legs, bare under stained, torn shorts, watched the flex and bunching of her rump as she danced to the rhythm of the fish, and wondered how it would move in that other dance that he longed to teach her—the dance to his rhythm. Her breasts were high, full and round, and he wondered how their weight would feel if they had no support but his own hands. Her mouth was wide and full, and he already knew her lips' intoxicating taste. Her eyes glowed with life, and he looked at her and imagined how they would look when he was inside her, when he had driven her mad, when she was drunk with the pleasure he knew he could give her.

He struggled to subdue his thoughts.

She caught four small fish in quick succession, and he dispatched each of them quickly and laid them on the grassy bank. "That's enough for dinner, I guess," she said.

"We will catch one or two more for Musa's dinner," Omar said, reaching for the rod. "He likes trout."

It was a case of bad timing. Jana moved to pass him the rod, and stepped down from the grassy mound she stood on onto a muddy spot. Her foot slipped. Off balance, she instinctively grabbed at Omar. But he was reaching for the rod, and as she jettisoned it, his own natural impulse was to reach to catch it. Caught off guard and off balance, and hampered by his wounded leg, Omar also fell.

Jana screamed a quick, involuntary protest. Omar half-turned as he fell, receiving her against his chest and wrapping his arms around her as they hit the little pool together.

It was icy cold. Jana gasped in shock and protest as the water surged up around her body, and immediately began to struggle to find her feet. But Omar, his arms around her, did not let go. He lay back in the water with Jana pressed to his chest, and his arms tightened.

"Omar!" she protested, as the icy water lapped at her back and her breasts pressed against his chest and the invigorating coldness—and his touch—turned her skin electric.

He didn't answer, and she stared into his face, tense with an unreadable expression. She took a slow, painfully expectant breath as he gazed into her eyes and she felt his hand shift to the back of her neck. Her heart pounded with hard, heavy beats. He held her without moving, gazing into her eyes as if looking for something there. His arms tightened around her, and his sea-green eyes got blacker and blacker as he gazed at her.

Jana's full wide lips, wet with the splash of waterdrops, unconsciously parted in expectation. Drops of water spangled in her eyelashes as the bright morning sun played down through the branches of the tree above.

She was filled with yearning, a deep, craving hunger she

scarcely recognized. She knew that he felt it, shared it—maybe it was even his own deep hunger that had communicated itself to her. His arms tightened to draw her more firmly against him as his head bent and his mouth came closer.

"Omar," she breathed.

As if the word had awakened him from a dream, he stilled. His hold stiffened. His eyes widened with an emotion that looked almost like fear. She saw and felt huge tension in him, and then his arms and his hands slowly, painfully, as if requiring every effort of conscious will, released her. She found her feet on the bottom. The icy water's touch was no longer sparklingly, electrically alive. She shivered once and clambered onto the bank.

His fishing rod had caught between the rocks a few yards away and he retrieved it, tossing it onto the bank before attempting to get out. His leg was obviously hampering him; she reached out a hand and he took it in an impersonal hold and struggled onto the bank. "Thank you," he said formally.

Jana futilely wrung out the hem of her muslin shirt.

His look now was impersonal. "We will go back now," he said calmly. "We have scared away the fish."

He began to wipe the rod carefully with a rag from the tackle box. He was gentle and careful with all the rod's nooks and crannies; there was a sexual imagery about it that made the air sharp. Jana bit her lip and dropped her eyes. Omar laid the rod down and replaced the tarpaulin over the rods and tackle box.

"Come, Miss Stewart," he said.

So he was going to pretend it had never happened. Jana looked up into his calm face and opened her mouth to say what she thought, but she quailed. What had happened, after all?

So she nodded, turned and meekly followed him back down the path. Below them the sun had reached the lake, and it sparkled invitingly, but Jana was too unhappily aware of her own inner feelings to be comforted by the beauty of the scene.

Her feet squished in her shoes, and she had to walk carefully. After a few minutes of careful concentration she took stock. She was very vulnerable here. Omar was a man of character. He was also a handsome, deeply attractive, deeply sexy man. Even in the freezing river, his touch had ignited a fiery heat in her. In that wild moment she would have given him whatever he asked her for, or whatever he had decided to take without asking.

But he had decided to take nothing. Perhaps he was being kind, saving her from what he knew to be his own passing interest. Maybe for him it was no more than the effects of sexual deprivation.

For her it was more than that. She loved Omar. She should have known it that morning when she heard his helicopter go down. And she was in danger of falling deeply, irrevocably in love with him.

That day Baba Musa and two companions turned up with several large sacks of charcoal and emptied them into a wooden bin on the verandah, and in the evening Omar produced a battered iron brazier from a shed and grilled the fish over charcoal.

It was delicious. The river trout had a more delicate flavour than the fish that inhabited the lake, and the charcoal grilling made them food for the gods.

"It's really wonderfully delicious!" Jana said.

The two princesses echoed, "It's wonderfully delicious, Baba!" and Kamala added, "Mommy likes them, don't you, Mommy?"

A profound silence fell upon them all. Jana blushed bright red, though there was no reason she should. Masha also blushed. Kamala merely looked at the faces around her with surprised interest for the fact that they were all staring at her.

"Shush, Kamala!" Masha protested.

Omar chewed, swallowed, and asked conversationally, "Who is Mommy, Kamala?"

Kamala blinked, and her eyes widened. Masha muttered to her, and she hung her head.

"I am waiting for an answer, Kamala."

"We were playing a game, Baba!" Masha supplied desperately. "It was because of Jalal the bandit!"

In spite of himself, he could not prevent a surprised smile. "How does Jalal the bandit come into it?"

Three voices at once jumped to explain. When the princesses saw that Jana had come to their defence, however, they immediately shut up and let her talk. "When the bandits were chasing us, I told Masha and Kamala that if we were caught they should pretend to be foreigners, to speak and understand only English. They decided that they would pretend they were my daughters, a very intelligent idea. Then they practised calling me Mommy. But you came and rescued us, so fortunately the game wasn't necessary."

Omar nodded, taking it all in. "And why do they call you Mommy today?" he asked, and that was unanswerable. Jana shrugged.

"Because it was such fun, Baba!"

"Running from the bandits was fun?"

"No, not that! But calling Jana Mommy—that is the English word for Mama, you know!"

"I am aware," Omar said, in dry appreciation of a masterly piece of manipulation by his own daughter.

"And we liked very much calling Jana Khanum Mommy instead of Jana Khanum, and that is what we do now."

Omar turned a raised eyebrow onto Jana, who shrugged. "Not to my face," she said.

"No, when we talk about her together! We just call her Mommy, it is our name for her in pri—in pri—"

"In private," Jana supplied.

"I see," said Omar grimly.

The next day, Baba Musa and Omar climbed into the Land Rover and disappeared for a couple of hours. When they returned they had certain supplies. Jana stared as they lifted two Uzi submachine guns out and carried them into the kitchen.

When Baba Musa left to take the princesses on another expedition, she found Omar in the kitchen, cleaning and checking the guns with the same careful attention he had bestowed on his fishing rod. There was a large box of ammunition.

"Where did you get them?" she asked.

"From my downed helicopter. It may be too close to Jalal down there—I wanted to take anything that might be useful to him."

Alarm signals were ringing in her brain, electric fear running up and down her spine. That was not his reason, she was sure. Or, not his only reason.

She said slowly, "I thought you said Jalal wouldn't be able to get past the foothills because the tribes up here hate him."

"Probably that's true. But it's better to be safe. Circumstances change. It may be that he makes a deal with a tribe, or takes a hostage...you never know."

Jana was silent, taking in all that he said, and much that he did not say. "If he can get as far as that, Jalal can get as far as this," she said, with ruthless precision.

He did not deny it. He looked at her as he wiped a cloth over the barrel of one of the guns. "Can you use a weapon, Jana?"

There was a long silence between them, as he measured her and she measured herself. "I've never handled one of these. My father taught me to shoot an ordinary rifle. Will you teach me?"

He nodded, satisfied. "It is not difficult." He stood and approached her, offering her the Uzi. He pulled a small metal box out of it. "Here are the bullets. You push them in so, and engage, so." The gun clicked. "Now you only push this lever, and you are ready to fire." He handed her the gun, and she took it, feeling instantly changed by the dangerous metal under her hands.

"One day soon I will take you out and you will practise," he said.

Jana turned troubled green eyes to his. "Omar, why doesn't Ashraf Durran come?"

"I do not know," he lied.

"How much danger is there that Jalal will come?"

"That also I do not know."

She had begun to fantasize and daydream, and the princesses calling her Mommy only added gas to the flames of her secret wishes. She knew that she had to get a grip on herself.

Easier said than done. It was one thing to get a cat back into a bag. There was another order of difficulty altogether when you couldn't find the bag. How had she managed to hide from herself for so long the truth of what lay behind her attraction to Omar? Now that she was aware of it, it seemed all-consuming. And now that love was added to the mixture, her sheer physical need for him had a potency that was at all times nearly overwhelming.

She couldn't pass within two feet of him without feeling the yearning pull of her need to touch him. She could not perform the simplest act, if he was watching her, without a heavy awareness of her own physicality.

If she was playing at the lake's edge with the princesses, or on the raft teaching them to improve their dive, she would feel her body grow heavy, her muscles would grow languid, and she would know that he had come out onto his balcony or the verandah and was looking at them.

She dreamed, but she had little real hope. Omar showed no sign of physical interest in her now. She thought that for him it must have been the simple combination of proximity and deprivation that had so briefly attracted him to her; if so, he was determined that it should never happen again.

She supposed she should be grateful. Her contract ended after a year. Probably it would be better for her if she did not leave Central Barakat as Prince Omar Durran ibn Daud ibn Hassan al Quraishi's cast-off mistress.

Twelve

"**W**hy has no one come?" Jana finally, desperately asked Omar.

The princesses had gone to bed. Jana and Omar were sitting working by lamplight, Jana stitching, Omar mending the rope that hauled up the refrigerator basket. Togetherness in the evenings was more dangerous than at any other time of day, but it was unavoidable. There was a limited supply of lamp fuel. They could not afford to waste it by lighting two rooms.

Omar paused. He had known the question must come, but he did not like the necessity of answering. "From the palace?"

"Yes, we sent those message flares the first night we were here! What is taking so long?"

He heaved a breath. "The problem is the message that was sent."

At the tone of reluctance in his voice, she turned and stared at him. "What do you mean?"

He tossed down the rope and straightened. "You remember I gave you three flares to fire?"

"Yes, and one misfired. But two went up brilliantly. He couldn't have missed them!"

"I am sure he did not. Two flares, however, means, 'All is well. Do nothing till further notice.'"

"Oh, my God," Jana breathed. Silence fell between them as she absorbed the information. At last she broke it with, "What would three have meant?"

"Three means, 'Emergency.' If he had seen three flares, Ashraf Durran would have come at once with a helicopter or trucks and sufficient armed men to dissuade Jalal from approaching."

"Oh, God!" she said again, her heart beating hard with nameless terrors. Not least of which was—how long could she live so close to Omar without telling him how she felt? "So—what happens now? We just wait here? For what?"

"I sent a messenger the next morning by Baba Musa. But the messenger had only a mule, and he must cross many miles of desert to reach the palace."

"Why didn't you *tell* me? I could have taken the Land Rover and been there in a day!" she demanded angrily.

"Jana, there is not sufficient fuel in the Land Rover to be sure even of reaching a gas station. You know this!"

"I would have tried!"

"It is for precisely this reason that I did not tell you. Because you are impulsive and headstrong, and if you had been determined to make so foolish and dangerous a trip I had not the strength to prevent you," said Omar.

"I think you should have let me go. Don't you think even on mule he would have reached the palace by now?"

"It is difficult to guess. It is very hot. Mountain people are not used to desert travel, and they are also not used to our concepts of time and urgency."

"I could still go."

"No," said Omar flatly. "It is too dangerous. Jalal knows we are still here. He would investigate every vehicle on the road."

She went on desperately, "My original plan was to start at night—that way I'd be safely past Jalal's territory before sunrise. I could still go. I could go tonight." She tossed aside the shorts. "I could leave in a couple of hours."

"Don't be a fool. Do you think he is such a primitive that he would not chase your lights?"

"The moon is almost full," she pressed. Suddenly, now that escape was possible, she saw how urgent it was that she get away. To stay here falling deeper and deeper in love with Omar was like committing slow suicide. "I could drive without lights. The road is so dark against the desert it would be possible."

He was losing his temper, and he knew that it was fatal to do so with her. He deliberately turned away and picked up the frayed rope. "The subject is closed," he said.

Jana flew up out of her chair. "What if your messenger doesn't make it? What if the mule died and he's on foot? What defence will we have if Jalal decides to come up here after us? I'm willing to take the risk! It's my own choice! I want to go!"

He got to his feet and stood over her. "Sit down and be quiet," he commanded, breathing to prevent his emotions rising to meet hers, to calm his already pounding blood. He could smell the perfume of her, sweet and heady.

"You—" she was saying. Her rounded lips were ripe and full, like a new peach. He knew that they tasted as sweet.

"I will not allow you to go!" he shouted. "Is that understood?"

"You have no right to keep me here!" Jana cried. She was so close to breaking that even with so little stimulus, her eyes sparkled with unshed tears. She lifted her hands and, without meaning to, he caught her wrists in an iron hold. She inhaled, lost her balance, and a step took her perilously closer to him. Her breasts were heaving, and through the neckline of the faded shirt she wore—his shirt—he saw their fullness and the line between the tanned skin and the pale. She wore no bra tonight, and the thought of cupping his hands around the soft, firm flesh assailed him, and how the weight of them would feel against his palms.

"No right? If he takes you hostage, what do you think he will demand for your return?" Omar demanded, burying his desire in fury. "Money from your father? That is not what he wants! He will demand concessions from me! Land, territory is what he wants! From me and from my brothers! His demand is for a share of the territory of the Emirates! Do you think I can afford to give him a hostage like you? You are here as a result of your own actions! You must suffer the consequences! Do not blame me!"

The touch of his hands was too much for her. Her anger abandoned her, and with a rush the empty space was filled with urgent, hungry need of him. Jana was trembling, weak with desire.

"I won't blame you, Omar!" she breathed, and her green eyes found his and he read pleading there. "I won't blame you for anything that happens!" And on the words his rage metamorphosed and he was consumed by the uncontrollable storm of need.

Her head fell back on her neck, unconsciously offering him her brown, smooth throat, and her voice was a moan that sent rivets of fire through him.

With a cry of despair, Omar released her wrists, pulled her roughly into his arms, and pressed his starving mouth against her perfect throat.

She cried out, an open-mouthed moan of relief and hunger, and her fingers threaded his hair, and he knew that it was inevitable now. He lifted his mouth and with his hand

in her loose hair, lifted her head and looked into her eyes.
"I will take you, Jana," he told her.

"Yes," she breathed, smiling and sighing as if she had
been waiting too long to hear the words. "Yes, Omar!"

He pressed his mouth to hers and then knelt on the thick
carpet at her feet and drew her down beside him. On their
knees in the flickering firelight he wrapped her in his arms
again and kissed her with wild, tender hunger. Her arms
enwrapped him, and he felt her complete surrender, and
shook with the assault of passion that rose in him.

They lay down, and he bent over her, admiring her
beauty in the soft light and shadow of the dancing, tossing
fire. "Will this bed be soft enough for you?" he asked. The
tenderness in his tone melted her, and she knew she was
safe with him.

She smiled and nodded. Her red hair was spilled across
the carpet under her head, glowing like melted copper. He
felt a confusion of feelings that almost swept him away.
Desire, passion and the deepest tenderness had invaded him
together.

First send a messenger to your wife, the prophet had
said. And when they asked, *What messenger?* he replied,
A kiss. A caress.

He did not know why the ancient saying arose in his
mind. He did not understand that it was because in his heart
he had made her his wife. But he bent over her with a joy
in his heart that was new to him, and although he had never
felt such powerful desire for any woman, his kiss on her
lips, on her cheeks and eyelids, was the whisper of spun
silk.

She was a feast, and he was deeply, ravenously hungry
for what she offered. To hold himself in check was a pain
that was pleasure to him. He kissed her face, and the palm
of the hand that stroked and clung to him, and then his
mouth crept softly down her curving inner arm to the tender
flesh at her elbow.

She was trembling with the lightest touch of his mouth against her skin, with the pressure of his hand locking her wrist in an inescapably firm hold. Above her elbow his mouth trailed over the soft worn fabric of his shirt hiding her flesh, to the tender nakedness of her throat and the soft vulnerable pulse of her neck, where he pushed the fabric aside to trail his lips down to her breast.

Slowly, gently, his hand moved between her breasts and he undid the shirt button by button before pulling it aside. Then he gasped at the sudden vision of her naked breasts, so round, so firm, so soft, and the already beaded pink of her perfect nipples.

Jana was alternately melting and shivering under the combined sensations of his soft lips and the brush of his beard on her skin. His hands were firm, strong and tender at the same time. She held his head, she opened her mouth under his passionate kiss when he kissed her. She kissed his hair when his mouth found her breast, she fell back with a hungry moan when he sucked on her nipples.

She cried out wordlessly, sounds of such hungry abandon that he felt his control going, and he covered her mouth with his kiss drunkenly, wildly, to smother the cries or drink them in, he did not know which. She flicked her tongue along his lips and it was a jolt of electric feeling that cut through him. His body surged against her thigh with promises that melted her again and again.

She was wearing his pants. He unbuckled the thick leather belt, unbuttoned the waistband, pulled down the zipper with a powerful sense of his possessive right to do so, and revealed the feminine softness of her belly and the curling mat underneath. Here, too, she wore no underwear, and she heard his breath catch hard in his throat. *"Janam,"* he whispered, but she was not sure about the last sound. Had he called her by her name, or by his own soul?

He stripped the pants down her legs and threw them aside, leaving her naked now except for the shirt that still covered her shoulders and arms. He dragged off his own shirt and jeans. Only the simple bandage wrapping his almost healed thigh covered him from her gaze, and she saw the planes and hollows of his body in firelight and knew she had never seen a more beautiful sight. Once before she had seen him nearly naked, but then his manhood had been hidden from her. Now it stood erect and strong, and she looked at it and felt a deep, primitive pleasure course through her. She put out her hand and grasped the hot, pulsing marble of him, and he closed his eyes and groaned.

His hand, too, found her centre. His fingers teasingly stroked her dampness, and his thumb sought carefully through the curling mass until her moan told him what he wanted to know.

She was so stirred, so filled with electric excitement, so passionately hungry, that this touch pushed her almost immediately over the brink into release. "Oh!" she cried, surprised by the suddenness of it, her curving eyes frowning with pleasure, and he watched greedily as her long legs shifted and her hips moved in the rhythm he had dreamed of creating in her.

And then he could wait no longer. His hand moved to push her thighs apart, and he raised himself up and lifted himself between her long legs, and his hard, hungry flesh sought the damp jungle of hers and pushed home.

She groaned, and he groaned with her, the sound of helpless submission to too much pleasure. For a moment he rested there, his elbows on each side of her head, and gazed down into her face with a hunger he did not understand.

Jana looked up into his dark eyes, black in the room of shadows and firelight, and at the need she saw there, the pleasure of his body in hers, she swooned and cried his name. She felt his flesh inside her leap in response, and cried out again as sensation stung her nerves with a hot honeyed tongue.

He began to thrust into her, hard, demanding, pounding

her with pleasure and with seeking. The seeking, his and hers, built in her, rising higher and higher towards a pitch of passionate need that was nearly pain. Her throat opened and he heard a song of yearning that pulled at his nerves, his heart, his whole being.

He could do nothing except thrust more strongly, more urgently as his own passion and desire consumed him, blinded him to all the world save her languorous eyes, her song of hunger.

He felt the same song in his own throat then, rasping, tearing its way out of him as he came closer and closer to what he sought in her. Then he found it, and a sun of pleasure seemed to explode simultaneously in his heart and his senses, burning, melting, blinding bright, sending light and heat to every cell of his being.

"Jana, *Janam!*" he cried hoarsely, giving himself up to her and to his pleasure in a way he had never experienced, for now he knew the secret. She was herself and his soul, and the soul of his soul. She was all things to him.

Thirteen

He did not know himself. He had been gentle with women before, he had feigned tenderness without knowing that it was false. He did not remember ever feeling tenderness in himself like this. He had scarcely believed it existed. Even for his daughters he had not felt this strange, fiery protectiveness that tore at his heart, and made him weak and strong in the same moment.

The fire had burned down now, it was glowing coals, like his passion for her. On the table the lamp also glowed, but its light, where they lay, only served to give them shadow.

He stroked the hair back from her forehead, touched her with his lips, caressed her still-damp skin. She had trembled in the aftermath, and wept, and he had kissed her tears on her cheeks, feeling that she wept for them both.

Though why they wept, he did not know.

They talked a little, softly, tentatively, about nothing in

particular. The night was cool, and with the death of the fire, she shivered.

"Come," he said, standing up and drawing her after him. Silently they pulled their clothes on and he led her to his own bedroom. There he wordlessly undressed her again and slipped beside her between the sheets. Then he drew her into his arms and kissed her gently, feeling his heart pulse with an emotion so unfamiliarly tender he might have wept himself.

Jana woke alone in the bed, stretched luxuriously, and smiled. She rolled over. Omar was standing at the open balcony door, gazing out. He was wearing a pair of loose white cotton trousers that tied at waist and ankles, nothing else, looking like a genie from a bottle.

"Good morning," she said.

He turned and looked down at her. "Good morning, *Janam*," he said, and with his use of that name a tension she hadn't known she was feeling let go. There was an expression that she had not seen in his eyes before.

She slid out from under the sheet and reached for the shirt she had been wearing last night. It lay strewn with the rest of their clothes on the bare wooden floor. Sliding her arms into the sleeves, she wrapped the flaps around her and went to stand beside him.

It was early; the sun was bright on the little goats on the hillside, just kissing the far edge of the lake, chasing the shadows across the water towards them. He wrapped one arm around her and drew her against his side, and she felt she had come home.

Nothing out of the ordinary happened that day, except that every time his gaze rested on her, her heart swelled. Whether she was cooking, or sweeping, or washing or singing, his eyes followed her with an expression of mingled surprise and possessive longing that made her glow.

The princesses were quick to notice the change, even if

they were not conscious of what they knew. Several times that day they called her Mommy, without seeming to be at all aware that they did so.

That night, as they washed the dishes, singing, Kamala said, with the wisdom of the very young, "Baba is happy."

It stopped him. He stood still with surprise, staring at his younger daughter, so that her eyes grew wide with alarm. "You are right!" he said at last, swooping on the child and swinging her up in the air in a way she had never before experienced, then wrapping her in his arms. "Baba is happy!" he told her.

Kamala giggled in delight, her eyes sparkling at him. "Me, too, Baba! Me, too," Masha cried. Then Prince Omar looked from one to the other of his daughters and learned that to love one person is to open your heart to all.

That night, Omar and Jana sat on the verandah and talked while they watched the stars appear in the lake. Here it had never been so easy as it had been at the palace for Omar to restrict the subject to business and politics and the rigidly impersonal. The atmosphere of the place was against him. Now, though, he found himself really *wanting* to tell her about incidents in his past, stories of the time before his father died. About childhood visits to this house, some of the happiest times he could remember.

"My mother did not come here with us. She was jealous, because this house was built for my father's first wife."

"What was her name?" Jana asked softly, so as not to break the mood. It was a beautiful, warm summer night without a cloud to obscure the stars and the brilliant three-quarter moon that glinted on the distant snow-topped peaks and on the lake. The same warm breeze stirred Omar's hair and played softly over her skin.

"My mother's name was Goldar," he said. "Of course, she had reason to be jealous. My father only loved one woman in his life, and everyone knew it."

Jana had meant to ask the name of his stepmother, the foreigner who had insisted on having somewhere she could get away from the palace formality and routine, which had of course been much stricter when she was a young bride. The much-loved wife for whom Sheikh Daud had built this house. But she did not say so. This kind of talking was new to him. She did not want to interrupt his flow, or perhaps make him uncomfortable about how much he was revealing to her.

"My mother was from Parvan," he continued, and lifted an arm out towards the mountains. "Parvan lies mostly there, beyond Mount Shir. We have a common border. The lower range, the Noor, is mine, but behind you see the higher peaks of the Shir range. They are in Parvan. My mother was cousin to the Shah of Parvan."

"Masha told me you fought in the war there."

"Yes," he said quietly.

"Is that why your father left you Central Barakat? Because it bordered on Parvan?"

He frowned. "Perhaps. I do not know his reasons."

"It was a dynastic marriage? You are a descendant of both royal houses?"

He glanced over at her. "Perhaps, although I am not in the immediate line of Parvan.

"My mother understood the situation when she agreed to the marriage, she knew why my father's agents proposed the marriage, but nevertheless she always hated my stepmother. And she believed that my stepmother favoured my brother Karim to inherit my father's throne. That is why she forced…"

He broke off.

"I suppose she thought that if you had an heir and your brothers did not your father might leave the kingdom to you?" Jana said quietly after a moment of silence.

She saw his jaw clench, his mouth tighten. "That is what she thought," he agreed, and bitterness was a dark thread in his tone. "My wife thought it, too. But she produced daughters. She was deeply distressed, though my father then was long since dead. She apologized to me after each birth, desperately, as if she had murdered all my hopes. I told her it was not so, that I would see that my daughter inherited my kingdom. I told her over and over that the fault was my own, that it is the man, not the woman, who determines the sex of the child. But she would not be consoled by science. She had no education except in religion."

Jana shook her head. What a terrible mismatch such a choice of wife must have been for such an intelligent, educated man! If she had learned one thing about him in the evenings of their conversations, it was how powerful and questing an intellect Prince Omar had. Even in English— his fourth language—he was formidable, and sometimes left her far behind.

But the most intelligent men did sometimes fall for beautiful bimbos, and if Masha and Kamala were anything to go by, their mother had been a beautiful woman.

"Your wife must have been very beautiful," she murmured.

"She was beautiful. Very beautiful. That is why my mother chose her for me. Of course when I first saw her, after the ceremony was complete, when her veil was taken down—of course I was enchanted with such beauty. It was only later, when I tried to speak with her, to make her my true companion, that I learned how little my mother understood me. It was too late then."

She felt desperately sorry for the young man who had been so disillusioned. And yet, he had renounced remarriage after her death. "You must have grown to love her," Jana murmured.

He flicked a glance at her. His face was warmly tanned now behind the neat black beard, but still in the darkness he looked like an Old Master portrait.

"Of course I loved her, she was my wife. I loved her as

my wife and the mother of my children,'' he said, knowing
as he said it that it was a lie. He had not known what love
was. ''But as a woman—I did not understand her. We had
nothing in common. We had no comfort to give each other
in difficult times, such as I saw between my father and
Azizah. My mother had not chosen me a companion, but
someone to produce an heir.''

''How old were you when you married?'' Jana asked,
wondering why he had submitted to the arrangement.

''I was eighteen.'' Jana gasped. ''She said it was my duty
to marry before I went to university in Russia, in case
something happened to me, and to leave behind me a pregnant wife. But my wife did not become pregnant. And only
two months after I went to Russia we were all summoned
home to my father's deathbed.''

A silence fell between them again. Then Jana said, ''I
suppose your mother was only treating you the way she
herself had been treated. She was married to your father
for one purpose only. I suppose she thought it was perfectly
all right to give you a wife for the same reason.''

He frowned and slowly turned his head. ''Yes...'' he
murmured, as the thought sank in. ''Yes, this is no more
than what was done to her. My father had a relationship
with Azizah that was loving and close, a true partnership—
but my mother had no such relationship with him—or anyone.''

''No great wonder that she was so ambitious for you.
Love had played so little part in her own life. How could
she feel it was important?''

He was silent, thinking, for a long time.

That night Omar went swimming with her. He took off
the bandage that wrapped his leg to disclose a raised, angry
red scar that was nevertheless well advanced in healing,
and they ran into the silky, moon-spangled water together

for the first time and struck out towards the middle of the lake.

He liked to swim; it was a relief to him to be in the water again, and his powerful stroke drew him quickly away from her. He swam till the tensions of lack of exercise had released and then he looked around.

She was standing feet apart on the raft, her arms up to squeeze the water from her long hair, staring up at the sky. In the moonlight her white bathing suit glowed as if with inner fire, and the shape of her was all curves, all female. His body grew hard in the water, in remembrance and anticipation, and he turned and swam towards the raft.

Jana did not hear his silent approach until he was hauling himself out. She turned, moonblinded, and gazed down at him. He lay on his back, his chest rising and falling rhythmically. His dark sea-green gaze was turned towards her, but she could not make out his expression.

"Take off your suit," he commanded softly.

Her stomach clenched with sudden sensual excitement. "Omar!" she protested on a laughing whisper.

All the lights down the valley had been extinguished long since. The house too was in darkness. There were only these two, and the stars and the moon.

"Take it off, *Janam*. Let me see your body."

Jana's eyes closed and her mouth opened, and her head fell helplessly back on her neck under the sensation his demand raised in her. Then she slipped one finger under one thin strap, and then the other, and peeled the white suit down off her body. She dropped it on the raft beside her.

"Stand closer to me," he commanded next, and she moved so that he could watch her from his position on his back.

The moonlight caressed her like a lover, outlining curves and hollows, highlighting her round smooth breasts, her cheek, her temple, her thigh, her belly. Underneath, the dark patch of curling hair was all mysterious, shadowed.

"Closer," he commanded. "Stand over me."

Her heart thumping, her body melting with the sparks that electrified every cell, she obediently stepped over him, straddling him, with one foot on either side of his waist.

He looked up at her for a long moment, the long legs, the white curves of her body, the hair made dark with wet, kissed by moonlight. His hands stroked up her legs as far as he could reach and his strong hands clasped her thighs, and as she shivered under his touch he gently guided her forward till she stood at his shoulder level.

"Kneel," he said.

"Omar!" she breathed helplessly, as raw sexual anticipation melted her womb.

"Kneel."

She knelt, one knee on either side of his head. His arms stroked up along her thighs and rump, and his hands encircled her waist, and then he drew her remorselessly down towards his waiting mouth. "Dance for me," he murmured, and then the heat of his tongue found that cluster of nerves that he had last night made the source of such pleasure to her.

She moaned. Her head drooped, her wet hair trailing down her back, sending drops of water over her heated, excited skin.

His mouth was wet and hot, and expert in the delicate game it played with her. His hands slid from her waist down over her buttocks, and his fingers slid between her thighs from behind and stroked the wet folds.

Jana fell helplessly forward onto her hands, and his grip encouraged the rhythmic motions that the buildup of desire dictated. Sensation ran along her skin, through her blood and nerves, as his mouth ruthlessly created the dance of her body that he wanted to feel.

It exploded suddenly, with a sharp, electrifying power that made her shudder, gasp, cry out, and press against him. In that moment he pushed his finger deep inside the soft infoldings, and another line of sensation rushed through her, meeting the first and exploding into ripples that seemed to go in all directions through her and the night sky.

Because she was the night sky. Its velvet was shot and sparked and spangled with shooting stars, and for one long, magic moment it seemed as if the dance of the stars would never end.

She moaned his name. His heart pounded at the sound, but he did not let her go until the dance was over.

Fourteen

"Lord." The private secretary, leaving the room after the usual morning consultation, paused and turned back. "Perhaps I should bring to your attention the matter of the man at the gates."

His Serene Highness Prince Rafi ibn Daud ibn Hassan al Quraishi, sitting in front of a mound of papers on his desk, looked enquiring. "Man at the gates? What is this?"

"A man speaking with the accent of the mountain tribes, Lord, arrived at the palace some days ago saying he had a message for Ashraf Durran from Prince Omar. When he was told that Ashraf Durran was not in the palace, he said that he had been entrusted to give it to no one but Ashraf Durran, and therefore he would await his arrival. He and his mule have settled down just beyond the gates."

Prince Rafi frowned. "Ashraf Durran is Cup Companion to my brother Omar, is he not?"

The secretary bowed. "I believe so, Lord."

"And he expected to find Ashraf Durran here?" Rafi sat for a moment, thinking. "Ashraf Durran has not set foot inside my territory in all the time since Omar stopped speaking to us. Why would Omar send to him here?"

His secretary, having no answer, merely stood silent. "Can it be that Omar is planning to make overtures of reconciliation? Has he sent Ashraf Durran on a mission that…but then why this tribesman with his message? Sent to intercept him?"

Still the secretary said nothing. "You'd better bring him to me, Samir." He stood up. "In the Tapestry Room. He will be more comfortable there."

A few minutes later the man entered the room, which, in the Barakati tradition, was furnished with carpets and cushions.

"Greetings, Rafi, son of Daud! May you always be strong!" he said, with the kind of polite salute that the mountain tribes accorded to their monarchs. After too much of the obsequious bowings and hand kissings of the so-phisticated city dwellers, Rafi always found this man-to-man attitude refreshing.

"Greetings, Aban of the clan of Bahram!" Rafi said. They sat, and Rafi called for cool sherbet drinks and sweet cakes to be served, for the mountain tribes were generous in hospitality and patient in business, and more would be learned from the man if his own code were not violated.

When the delicacies had been consumed, and Rafi knew that the time was right, he observed, "You have my brother Omar's trust, Aban of Bahram."

"May I be worthy of it," said Aban, with a fierce, bristling look that told Rafi he had to deal with a man of certain honour.

"We have not the pleasure of entertaining Ashraf Durran at the moment. Did my brother Omar tell you when he expected his Cup Companion to visit?"

Aban smiled. "But it is summer, Lord! It is well known

to all the tribes that the royal party comes to the mountains in summer. This has been a tradition of your own father, peace be upon him, and his fathers before him for many generations. Therefore I sought Ashraf Durran here and now await his arrival.''

Rafi sighed and nodded as the mystery became apparent. ''Where was my brother Omar when he gave you the message?'' he asked.

''He did not himself give me the message, being wounded. Musa of our tribe gave it to me, in our village near Lake Parvaneh. 'Take it to the palace and give it into the hands of none other than Ashraf Durran,' he said. I shall do so.''

Rafi sat forward. ''Wounded? My brother Omar? How?''

Aban frowned evilly. ''The villain Jalal, the bandit of the desert, who makes travel to the city difficult for our people, he shot down Prince Omar's *halikuptar,* Rafi son of Daud.''

''Shot him down!'' Rafi cursed. ''Who tended him?''

''Doktar Amina visited him.''

''That at least is good news. And is he well? He recovers?''

''As to that, Lord, I do not know. For I departed with my message on the morning after the fireworks.''

''There were fireworks?''

The tribesman lifted his arms. ''Two great fireworks went off in the sky on the night that Prince Omar was wounded.''

''Two?'' Rafi frowned in perplexity. Omar's first message, then, was *All is well.* ''And then—the next morning, you were sent.'' To himself he muttered, ''It doesn't make sense.''

The two men were silent for a moment. Then Prince Rafi said, ''Aban of the Bahrami, I have told you that Ashraf Durran is not here with us, nor do we expect him. Undoubtedly you will find him at the palace of my brother Omar, by the River Sa'adat. This is many days' march from here, I know, and you have already walked many days. Therefore I will send you to Ashraf Durran with the message in my *halikuptar*. Your mule will be cared for here until your return.''

''Prince Rafi is kind,'' said Aban, bowing, and admirably concealing his reaction to the prospect, whatever it was.

''But I make one request of you, Aban Bahrami. I ask to read my brother Omar's message before you leave, in case he gives some news of Jalal the bandit.''

Aban of the Bahrami thought for a moment. ''You will return the message to me, that I may deliver it safely?''

Rafi gave his assurances, took the message, read it, returned it. Then, concealing his agitation from the tribesman, he thanked him and put him into the hands of Samir.

Two hours later, Aban of the Bahrami tribe was taking his first ride in a *halikuptar*. The story of his adventures would warm many a winter's evening in future.

Long before that, Rafi was on the phone to Karim.

''It's beautiful,'' she breathed. ''It's the most beautiful thing I ever saw. Who on earth made it?''

He had taken her into the mountains to teach her to shoot the Uzi, and now, on their return, as if to make them both forget what might be necessary, he had led her into the bedroom. There he had opened the safe and lifted out a carved box of some beautiful wood.

It was a pedestal cup, wrought of pure gold and precious gems—cabochon rubies and emeralds the size of grapes studded all around the rim, smaller ones studded around the pedestal, and flat-cut emeralds and rubies making up the body of the bowl. Smaller faceted gems encircled the large ones. All were held together with gold. Even without being held up to the light, the colours glowed and glittered. Held up to the light it was pure magic.

''It was made by the best court artisan, many centuries ago, for my ancestor Jalal. It is called the Cup of Happiness,

Jahmeh Sa'adat, or *Jahmeh Jahn,* the Cup of the Soul,''
Omar told her. ''The legend is that whoever owns the cup
will find true happiness.''

There was something in his voice as he said it. Jana
glanced up. ''The magic didn't work so well for you,'' she
suggested.

He did not reply.

She gazed down at the magical thing in her hands. It
seemed to have an aura of power—it made her hands ache
slightly to touch it.

''Is it safe here?'' she asked.

''During my cousin's war I was offered much money for
this cup. I think there are those who would steal it if they
could.'' She thought of the missing treasures in the palace
and wondered how many treasured things he *had* sacrificed
to help finance his cousin's war.

''My brother's seal was taken from his own treasury. But
no one save myself knows where this is kept. And now
you. For that reason it is perhaps safer here than at the
palace.

''I keep it here at Lake Parvaneh because this is where
I was happy, even though it was many years ago. Here the
promise of the cup was not such a lie as elsewhere.''

''Is that why this place became your hideout? Because
you could remember happier times here?''

''Perhaps. I came because it was the one place where I
could be alone. Away from the reminders of what my life
had become.''

He looked at her. There was so much that he wanted to
say to her, but he could not find the words. He wanted to
ask her what it meant when she looked at him, as she did
now, but he did not know how.

''But you were already too alone,'' she observed.
''Weren't you?'' She gazed thoughtfully at the beautiful
cup between her hands.

''What do you mean, Jana?''

"Not many people find happiness in pure solitude over the long term. Most of us, when we say happiness, we mean other people. We mean love. Don't we?" She looked up at him, but her words had caused a kind of shock in him that left him unable to respond.

"Do we?" he asked at last.

She didn't answer directly. "You lost your father, your stepmother, your own mother, your wife, even the Grand Vizier…and you're alienated from your brothers, isn't that right? And you fought your cousin's war and saw many die. And all that loss happened within the space of ten years?" He said nothing. "It must have seemed like blow after blow for a very long time."

"Solitude comforts me," Omar said, realizing only as he said it that it was no longer true. It was not solitude that comforted him now. Perhaps it had never truly comforted him, but only that, somehow, in solitude, his nameless yearning was less urgent.

"Solitude has a lot of things going for it. One of them, when you've suffered loss, is the knowledge that in solitude at least you're not going to lose anyone, because there's no one to lose."

His heart contracted as the shafts of truth pierced it. She was right. He had retreated to solitude because… Wordlessly he lifted the cup from her hands as she offered it to him, wrapped it and restored it to its beautifully carved and gilded box. He put it back in the safe and locked it.

From the shore of the lake, the cries of his daughters, playing with friends from the village, carried on the breeze. For a moment they both listened, and then Jana looked at him with a smile. She said nothing, but she did not need to say anything. He knew he had never heard his daughters sound so carelessly happy in all their young lives. He knew, too, that it was not only the companionship of friends, but also of himself and of Jana, that made them so happy now.

Together they moved out of the room and down to the

kitchen, where they began the preparations for lunch. Omar found pleasure in the simple shared task. Today, for the first time, he examined himself and understood that the pleasure was not only in the "simple," but also, and very importantly, in the "shared."

"How many are we today?" he asked, pulling down plates to put on the table.

"I think it's only Amir, Peroz and Maysun, but maybe you'd better check."

He went out onto the verandah to do a head count, and thought, *She is right. There is pleasure I did not find before in fatherhood.*

When he returned to the kitchen, he said, "Two more have joined. Zandigay and one whose name I do not remember. Do we feed them all?"

"There's plenty of soup and *naan*," Jana said, for she had learned the country custom of leaving a large black pot permanently on the back of the stove, and pouring into it all the stock from boiled vegetables and most of the leftovers, so that there was always soup to be had.

Obediently Prince Omar laid the table for nine.

"Omar," she said, after a moment.

"Jana?"

"Will you tell me sometime how you came to be estranged from your brothers?"

He stood for a moment in silence, his hand wrapped around half a dozen soup spoons. "Yes, I will tell you," he said.

From the first time of meeting her, he had spoken to Jana as he had to no other woman. To no other person. He had found himself telling her truths and secrets about himself, his life.... Once he had recognized what was happening, it had taken rigorous control to prevent himself telling her everything about him, as if she were his dearest friend, chosen for him by fate... He had talked about politics and the economy, but in his heart he had been telling her his griefs and joys, his triumphs and disasters.

He had had such freedom only with one other woman— his stepmother. That beloved foreigner who had been his father's closest adviser as long as he had lived. She had died when Omar was already deeply unhappy, leaving him with no one.

In this house he could no longer keep up the facade with Jana. Now if he opened his mouth to talk about politics, that was not what came out. He told her those secrets of his deepest heart, they spilled out of him uncontrollably. He was like a man who has been wandering in the desert for days and stumbles upon fresh water in an oasis.

But there was one thing he could not say to her. If the cup's promise held true, he would be happy. But the cup was a legend, no more. If he spoke to her of what was deepest in him, he might hear that the cup had no power to give him happiness, now or ever again.

Their first priority in the case of attack had to be the safety of the princesses. They discussed it between themselves, and then with Baba Musa, and made plans. These plans had to be communicated to the children.

"I wish we didn't have to tell them," Jana worried. "It seems so sad to break the magic by worrying about an attack that might never happen."

"They are princesses," he said. "They lead privileged lives. There is a price to this, Jana, and it will be well if you understand it. They are not Western children who can be cosseted and protected from life. There is a price that they pay, and they will always pay it."

She knew he was right. "But don't be any harder than you have to," she begged.

But the princesses took it as their father expected them to take it. He told them briefly of the danger, more fully of the plan to get them to safety if it happened.

"Can you do it, Masha?" he asked.

"Yes, Baba," the little princess said stoically.

"Can you do it, Kamala?"

"Yes, Baba."

They never mentioned it again in Jana's hearing.

Because of his doubts, his tenderness gave way to a wild, demanding passion. He could not be sure of her, he could not ask what he both feared and desired to know, but everything he asked of her sexually, she gave, and everything he gave sexually, she accepted. He was sometimes ferociously passionate with her, sometimes wildly imaginative, and in her repeated cries of pleasure and surprise he found the comfort his soul sought.

That night was very hot, a heat more of the desert than the mountains. He awoke with the torment on him. He got up, dressed and went to her bedroom, where the heat had made her restlessly kick off the heavy linen sheet. At the sight of her bare legs he had to resist the temptation to strip off again and simply make love to her here.

With a whispered kiss he woke her.

"Get dressed," he murmured. "Come with me."

Jana was helpless to resist such a plea. She dreamed of him constantly, and when he woke her, her womb instantly began to melt in anticipation of what he would do to her, what pleasure she would experience before the dark look in his eyes had been assuaged.

She dressed in what clothes were nearby and silently followed him out of the house. Tonight he headed for the river, and they silently began the climb up the river path. For twenty minutes by starlight they walked, until they reached the little pool where they had fished. The three trees bending over the pool were ghostly shapes in starlight. There was no moon tonight.

Jana stopped when Omar did. She was breathing heavily,

was sweating from the long climb in such unusual night-time heat.

He looked at her, his body instantly growing hard at the sight of those high breasts, the long legs, the thought of how he would touch them, how he would enter her, how she would respond. "Take off your clothes," he said.

Such commands as this always made her melt with instant desire. She wordlessly began to strip as he hungrily watched, holding himself back from touching her, because when he resisted the pleasure was always greater. When she was naked in the faint light he undressed himself. Then he held out his hand.

"Omar, it'll be freezing!" she protested on a laugh.

He shook his head. "That is why," he said, and the promise of unknown pleasures made the air shimmer. After a breathless moment when she could hardly breathe, she put her hand in his and he led her down into the little shimmering pool.

It was freezing. The temperature difference between air and water was staggering. She felt her breasts contract, her nipples harden, her skin electrify as he led her into the water and drew her down. Jana gasped and panted. "Oh, it's so cold!" she said, laughing breathlessly.

He drew her to him, and she felt his sex hard against her thigh. A second later he had pushed into her, his sex cold against her inner heat, so that she gasped with the unexpected sensation. He thrust hard into her, standing on the bottom and holding her waist firmly, drawing her down onto his sex with hard, rhythmic pulses, and her heat and his own warmed his flesh.

She moaned as familiar sensations coursed through her blood and nerves, and then, suddenly, he lifted her free of his body. A helpless moan protested her loss, but another part of her went instantly tense with anticipation as with his hand he found the hard knot of pleasure waiting to be released, and he stroked that.

There were too many sensations. The burning heat that his stroking fingers raised in her centre, the current of icy water on her skin, the hunger in his dark eyes as he watched for every sign of pleasure in her…suddenly the burning heat spiralled up into electric joy and she cried the news of her first release.

She knew Omar now, and she knew that there would be more.

The next second he was thrusting inside her again, and again his manhood was cold, and the shock against her heated system was incomprehensible to her senses. He thrust hard and harder, and it seemed to her that the starry blackness of the night invaded her inner being, that she was starry night within and without, and in both places the stars wheeled and sang and thrilled her being.

She lost her sense of time and place and self, she was only this strange, wild mix of sensation, cold, heat, burning that melted everything…she cried and moaned uncontrollably, her cries drunken, mad. He would pull out of her to chill his body in the water, meanwhile driving her to release with his hand, and then thrust his cold flesh back into her overheated centre.

"Omar!" she begged once, when it seemed too much, when she scarcely knew anymore that pleasure was a separate thing from existence.

"Do you like it, *Janam?*" he panted, driving into her.

She was helpless. A gasp of laughter escaped her. "Yes!" she cried. "Yes, I like it. I love it. Oh, Omar, what you do to me…"

"You love it?" he demanded ferociously. "You love it?"

He was dragging her down against his body, thud, thud, thud, and only just keeping control of his own pleasure. "I love it," she cried, though in her heart the last word was changed. Not *it,* she wanted to say. Not *it,* Omar. But even in the madness of total pleasure, even though she did not remember why, she did not allow the word *you* past her heart.

"I love it," he growled. "I love it, *Janam.*"

From the depths of her sexual self, an overwhelming wave of pleasure rose up, and shook her so desperately she was nothing but a leaf on the tree that was Omar's sex. Then she cried like an animal, from the deepest part of her, in raw, crude gasps as he thrust into her. Everything—her body, the water, the tree, the sky, the stars, and Omar, seemed to her drugged, electrified senses to be her own nerves overwhelmed with pleasure. Everything exploded around her and in her in a series of wild shocks, and her throat was torn by high wordless cries of surprise.

He had not meant to go with her, but her response now was too much for him. He had never heard that note in her cries before, the cry of simultaneous destruction and renewal. He exploded wildly, uncontrollably; he too felt the cries of completion torn from his throat, and he experienced a pleasure too wild to live. He thrust into the heat of her sex until his legs dissolved and gave way, and the water closed over them both.

She seemed to black out. She remembered nothing but blackness and stars, and then she was lying on the grassy bank, shivering, Omar beside her.

"Omar!" she pleaded. "Omar, what are you doing to me?"

He stroked her wet hair from her temples and forehead. That he could give her so much pleasure assuaged him briefly. He could not explain what it was he wanted from her. He could not explain what drove him.

She raised herself on an elbow. The wind that blew over them was so hot her body had already stopped shivering. "It is the wind from the desert," he said.

He was hard again. He stood up, his long body pale in the starlight, and gazed down at her and knew that he could never get enough of her if he spent a lifetime loving her.

With a sleepy, drugged smile she saw him above her. He had destroyed her, he had created the wildest of passion in her and then sated that passion, but there was one hunger that had never been quenched. It was a hunger new to her, created out of the storm of the passionate joy he gave her, and now, as she looked at his engorged flesh, she understood herself.

Her sleepy, half-lidded eyes moved from his manhood to his face. "Stand over me," she commanded.

He frowned in surprise. "What?"

Impatiently, she pulled at his left foot. He lifted it and put it on the other side of her, so that his legs straddled her. She lay back again, staring up at him. Even now, totally sated, she felt faint with the promise of pleasure in that proud instrument.

"Kneel," she said.

He gasped as though he had been punched. *"Janam!"*

"Kneel."

He could not resist. He knelt, and her hand came up and encircled his sex, and drew him down towards her smiling mouth. She licked her lips. He watched and trembled, and then she guided him into her mouth.

He had never allowed a woman to do this to him. Had he feared his own loss of control? He could not remember. He only knew that he was helpless to resist the pleasure now.

He fell forward on his hands, groaning her name, half in protest, half in excitement.

"Janam, Janam, *Janam!"*

Now it was she who built his passion, she who controlled his pleasure. Her tongue caressed him in a thousand magic ways, her teeth nibbled, her mouth opened wide for him while he grunted and cried out his passionate surprise.

She reached up, and her hands grasped the lean hips, and led his body in the search for pleasure. She pulled him in again and again, with little grunts of satisfaction, while he arched his neck and cried his uncontrollable joy aloud. It was true, what he feared: this went too deep, this stripped him bare. He was a shorn lamb exposed and burning in the hot wind of desire.

It tore through him then like a black wind, uprooting everything, blasting everything. He felt the suddenness in every cell, the pleasure in every muscle, and his body leapt and shuddered uncontrollably. But she knew him too deeply to lose him now. She kept him in the heat of her mouth and wrapped her arms around his hips, and tasted the salt of his joy.

"How the hell did it happen?" Prince Karim's voice shouted down the wires.

Rafi shrugged. "Every mountain man knows you have to be crazy to live in the desert in summer. They also know that Sheikh Daud's court used to come up to the mountains every May."

Karim frowned. "They *also* know that Sheikh Daud is dead and the kingdom divided!"

Rafi only smiled. "Karim, you know the way of the tribes. It wouldn't occur to them that you don't all still come and join me in my palace in summer."

"I don't understand why he wasn't told to go to the palace on the river!"

"Maybe he was. People hear what they expect to hear. Who knows how the message got distorted?"

"So Aban sat there with his mule for how long, waiting?"

"My people say they saw flares in the sky some time ago. No one is certain how long he's been sitting outside the gates. But it's a long walk through the mountains from Lake Parvaneh."

Karim groaned. "But there were unquestionably two flares?"

"Everyone is agreed, there were two flares."

"'All clear. Take no action until further notice.'"

Rafi made no reply.

"But the next day he sent a message to Ashraf telling him he's been wounded and to send transport to get them all out of there and watch out for Jalal."

"It's possible his condition worsened during the night."

"If that's the case, Rafi, he's probably dead." Karim cursed.

"Doktar Amina saw him," Rafi pointed out.

"I heard that, and I also heard you say he sent the message the next morning asking for urgent help. To me, that says that something happened during the night. Like he had internal bleeding she didn't catch or something."

"We still have to get the girls out. And this teacher."

"If I get my hands on the teacher..."

"Save your venom for Jalal," Rafi advised.

Fifteen

He lay beside her, stroking her face, her arm, her hair. He had been stripped bare, she had made him naked, and now he knew himself.

"No woman has done what you have just done for me," he murmured.

Jana smiled, and he watched the stars glimmer in her eyes. "I've never done it before, either."

She felt the sigh of satisfaction in him. "No, my heart?"

He kissed her gently, and they lay in each other's arms without speaking, stroked by the soft grass and by the warm desert wind, gazing lazily up at the stars. Minutes went by while they lay there, and peace pervaded their spirits.

"Did you used to swim here as a child?"

"Yes, it was our favourite place."

"You and who else?"

"Karim and Rafi. My brothers." There was silence while the warm wind blew.

"You must miss them," Jana said at last.

"Miss them?"

"I remember watching you on television a few years ago. I remember thinking how the three of you seemed to be…just…" She paused, searching for her meaning.

"Seemed to be?" he prompted her. In this moment, speaking of them to her, he suddenly missed his brothers very much.

"Connected, I guess. It was just so nice to see you all looking as though you really loved each other and got on well together."

"We did. We were. Or so it seemed then."

"You were so gorgeous, too! I was at university, and we all watched in the common room—the girls were all crazy about you and saying which one they'd pick."

He leaned up over her on one elbow and gently stroked her smooth stomach. "Which did you choose?" he asked.

Her enchanting smile glinted up at him. "Then, or now?"

He kissed her.

After a moment she asked, "Will you tell me about your brothers?"

He found he wanted to tell her. Omar released her to lie back, and crossed his arms under his head. "It goes back. This bandit, Jalal, who is now so entrenched in my territory—I knew he would be trouble from the beginning."

"What was the beginning?"

"He sent us a message when we came into our inheritance, stating that he had a right to a share of the kingdom, and demanding a meeting with us."

"What did he think gave him the right?"

"He did not specify. He is descended from a notorious bandit who controlled much of the desert in the last century. No doubt that is his reason."

"He never told you?"

"We never met with him."

Surprise brought her upright, and she stared down at Omar in the starlight. "What? Why not?"

"Because to meet with a man like this already gives legitimacy to his demands. People would say, 'Well, they have talks with him, there must be some truth in his claims.' And before you know it, you are the oppressor. As long as we do not talk to him, Jalal the bandit remains a bandit."

Jana lay down again. "It seems pretty futile to me. How can you sort anything out if you don't talk to him?"

"By battle, of course. This is what I urged on my brothers. Long before Jalal had gained the strength of numbers he now has, I urged them to mount a joint campaign to go and destroy his headquarters and drive him out."

"And they didn't agree?"

"They thought he was a small man who would go away if deprived of attention. They said to fight with him would be as bad as to meet with him. It would give him legitimacy. The Grand Vizier was then ill, and did not give firm advice. So Karim and Rafi won. And so we missed our chance."

"And is that when you stopped talking to your brothers?"

He was silent for a long moment without realizing it, as scenes from the past played in his head. Good and bad. He had forgotten how many happy memories there were.

"No," he said at last. "No, it was not then. A couple of years later we heard of Jalal again. When I returned from the war in Parvan I had a force of seasoned fighters—what was left of them," he added, and she knew the war was another terrible memory. "Jalal had taken up residence in my territory, and he was pressing his demands. I said to my brothers again that we should...they agreed, but they kept on delaying the date, and finally—I was angry with them—I went myself, with a small force of veterans. He was in my country, after all. I put his fortress under siege, hoping to starve him out. It didn't work.''

''Why not?''

''He was somehow getting supplies in without our discovering how.'' He shrugged. ''We should have attacked. But there were so many women and children inside—the place is like a village, not a military camp. We had seen so much vicious fighting from the Kaljuks against my cousin's people…all my men had had enough of such things. We abandoned the siege.

''And then I returned to the palace, unsuccessful, to find that Faridah my wife was dead. She was taken ill in her pregnancy, and refused to go to the hospital. And not one of my staff had the courage to countermand her in her delirium. She and the child were lost. They told me it was a boy. Poor Faridah! She died knowing that her son died with her.''

''Oh, Omar, what a terrible story,'' Jana said softly.

''I never spoke to my brothers again,'' he said.

They lay in silence, with the night all around them. A star fell.

''Would Faridah have lived if it had been a joint mission?'' she asked.

Omar frowned. ''I don't understand your meaning.''

Jana rolled over and propped herself up on her elbows. It was lovely to lie naked in the cool grass like this, on a perfect night, talking. She wondered absently if a more perfect moment could exist in life than what she was blessed with now. Omar caught a lock of her hair in his fingers and tickled his mouth with it.

''I am just wondering why you blame your brothers so totally when it seems that you would have been away laying siege to Jalal's fortress whether they had come along or not,'' she said gently. ''It seems to me it was just a thing of bad timing.''

''It *was* bad timing. Very bad timing,'' Omar said

grimly. "If they had not delayed, we would have been finished before Faridah fell ill."

"Or if you had waited for them, you wouldn't have started yet," she pointed out mildly, and was totally unprepared for his reaction.

He went completely still. He seemed to stop breathing; he looked as if even his heart had stopped beating. He lay for a frighteningly long moment, the lock of her hair caught in his motionless hand, his eyes unseeing, all his vision turned inward.

"Omar, I'm sorry!" she breathed. Never had her thoughtless impulsiveness been so badly timed.

He held up a hand to stop her. "No," he said quietly. "No. You are right. It is not my brothers who were to blame. It was myself."

"Oh, Omar!"

He sat up, drawing his knees up, and rested his arms on them. "And it is not my brothers whom I hate. It is myself," he said, with the flat tones of certainty.

"Oh, God!"

He was speaking slowly, more to himself than to her. "I did this to her. I and no one else. I was away and she became ill. I was the only one who could have taken her to the hospital against her wishes. Ashraf, perhaps, if he had been there, but he was with me. Our Grand Vizier, but he was dying himself. If I had not been so angry with my brothers for what I saw as—" He looked into her eyes. "You see, *Janam,* I thought the delay was another excuse, a prelude to them saying, oh, well, not now, another time! And so, in a fury, I went alone. It was foolish, and useless."

She could say nothing. The words poured from him, tumbling out in the way that such discoveries are made. "It was not them, it was myself. I robbed my wife of the one thing she wanted in life—she wanted to bear a son! She would have been happy then, she would have loved a son as she had never loved anyone. Instead of this, she died. I think she died without ever having been happy.''

''I'm so sorry,'' she whispered helplessly, kneeling beside him, her hand on his shoulder.

''I could not make her happy, *Janam.* I told you that she disappointed me. But I also disappointed her. What beautiful young woman marries without hoping to love? But I could not make her happy. I tried. When I came home from the university in Russia…but I could give her nothing. Not even a son.''

He was silent for a long time. Then he looked into her face, and by the faint light she saw that his eyes and cheeks were wet. ''You have stripped me naked in every way tonight, *Janam,*'' he whispered. ''No wonder I call you my soul.''

She could do nothing but shake her head helplessly and kiss his shoulder. In response he took her hand and buried his mouth in the palm.

''I am flawed, *Janam,*'' he said hoarsely. ''I do not know how to make a woman happy.''

''We have to go up there first and get them out,'' Karim argued.

''I agree,'' said Ashraf Durran.

Both Prince Karim and Omar's Cup Companion had flown to Rafi's palace with all possible speed. As usual, between the princes there was disagreement over how to act. Karim wanted to mount a rescue operation as a first priority. But Rafi, worried because there was only landing room for one helicopter at the house at Lake Parvaneh, wanted to mount a much larger operation. Ashraf agreed with Karim, and he was privately determined not to wait beyond the next morning, whatever the disagreements of the two princes.

''We might as well do for Jalal on the way in,'' said Rafi again.

"That might take a week. Rafi, we have to know what the situation is up there. How do we know Jalal hasn't taken the kids hostage?"

"We'd have heard. He'd have sent his demands before now. But if he has, what is the point in going up there with one helicopter? We'd only be ambushed before we found out anything, and give Jalal two more hostages."

"We have to know whether Omar is alive or dead. If he's alive and in a bad way the most important thing is to get him to the hospital, and we'll do that a lot faster if we're not simultaneously engaged in tank warfare."

Rafi shook his head. "I still think that to go in with one helicopter would be insane, especially if Jalal *has* managed to get up there and take the place over."

"Only one can land at the house, but there's room to put a couple more down on the far side of the lake if necessary."

"Necessary, but useless. I think we should go in overland with a reasonable force, even if we don't take on Jalal en route."

"If he *is* still alive, Omar won't thank us for invading his sovereign territory with our armies without his leave! Damn it, Rafi, will you think for a minute!"

Rafi raised a finger. "Right. You're right. We want to heal the breach, not cause a new one."

"Look, it's simple—Ashraf, you and I go in a couple of small choppers capable of landing near the house. We take a couple of Sikorskys with troops. They can hover and keep us covered while one of us lands and checks out the situation. If necessary, troops can be landed by parachute. If not, we evacuate the girls, Omar and Ms. Stewart."

"I don't like it," said Rafi. "I'd rather hammer Jalal's positions now and…"

"Wherever that is," Karim pointed out.

Ashraf Durran intervened at last. "Every time the issue of Jalal comes up, you all seem racked with indecision.

What is so difficult about this, Prince Rafi? It is absolutely clear to me that the first priority is to go in with a rescue and get the princesses and Omar and Jana Stewart out. Whatever we do about Jalal, that is and remains an absolute priority. I myself will go in at dawn tomorrow, whatever you decide to do."

"Ashraf is right. We can't sit here arguing all day. We've got to do something," said Karim.

"All right, all right," said Rafi. "You're right. We fly in, we fly them out. We take a couple of backup helicopters to cover us in case Jalal feels like repeating himself by shooting us down."

"We go at first light," said Karim.

They made their way back to the lake in-silence. Jana wanted to speak, but was afraid. Omar was too full of thought to notice the silence.

As usual, they went to their own bedrooms. Omar threw off his clothes and lay down on the bed, but he did not fall asleep. There was still so much to think about, so much to sort through. She had made him see so many things that he had been unwilling to see before.

But now he had to look at them. His future depended on his ability to face the truth about himself.

He had lied to himself, and out of the worst motive: out of fear. He had blamed everyone but himself for the void his life had become, but in secret he had always blamed himself.

His mother had inveigled him into a marriage that was a terrible mistake both for Faridah and himself, but he had tried to make that marriage work. He had felt it his duty to make his wife happy. He had tried, first, to educate her, but she would not submit. She had learned large parts of the Koran by heart, and she had honestly believed that that was the best education a woman could have. In vain had he tried to make her feel that more was required of her mind, in vain had he tried to interest her in any science or art.

Nor was she interested in helping him to rule the country that would one day be his. She had wanted only one thing to be complete: to produce a son. And because of him she had never succeeded.

He had felt an even more bitter betrayal in her death than in his marriage. Her unhappy death stamped him a failure. He had never been able to make her happy. He had not succeeded in truly loving her. Perhaps if he had been able to love her, she would not have died.

That was why he had said he would never marry again. He had not realized it until now. He was bitterly afraid of failure. That was what prevented him from knowing and declaring his true feelings for Jana. Fear. He had been raised a warrior, but fear had dictated his life.

No more.

Sixteen

He heard the faint but telltale beating of wings as the sun came up, and went out onto the balcony. They were coming from the southeast, still far in the distance. He could not see the markings.

Jana joined him. She was calm but worried. "Who is it?" she asked him.

"Only two possibilities," Omar said. "Ashraf Durran, or—"

He paused. "Or Jalal?" she asked firmly, and her bravery smote his heart. What a woman she was! No need to fear that she would weaken if it was the bandit!

"It's possible some foreign country or militant group has armed him," he admitted. "We'll be able to see in a few minutes. If it's Ashraf the markings will be obvious."

"I'll get the girls dressed," she said. Those plans, soberly discussed with the princesses, as to what they would do if Jalal found a means of attacking them at the lake—it wasn't going to be easy to carry them out.

As if on cue, the two princesses, still in their pyjamas, burst into his bedroom. "Baba! Baba!" they cried. Seeing the room empty, they stopped.

"We are here, children," Omar called. Their relief on seeing their father and Jana Khanum on the balcony was palpable. They dashed out, excited and afraid.

"*Halikuptar!*" shouted Masha.

"Yes, we are watching them now," Omar said calmly.

Masha took a deep breath, then bravely asked, "Who is it, Baba?"

"I don't know. Therefore you must go with Jana Khanum now and get dressed quickly."

"Yes, Baba."

"Baba, I'm frightened," said Kamala. "What if it is Jalal the bandit and his bad men?"

"Then you will go to Baba Musa in the village and pretend to be his granddaughters until I can come and rescue you," he said firmly. "We will all do exactly as we planned."

"Oh, Baba! I am so afraid!" A sob threatened in Kamala's voice.

"Bravery is to be afraid and still to do what is right, Kamala. You are a princess. Always remember that."

"Yes, Baba." The resolve to be strong like her father was evident in the way she drew in her breath and straightened her small shoulders. Jana's heart was breaking for her, but this was no time for softness. The children had to escape what might be coming if at all possible, and only courage and obedience would serve them now.

The princesses obediently turned away, and Jana went quickly with them to their room, where she got out the well-worn village costumes that had been acquired for this moment and helped them to dress. Then she herself hurriedly threw on jeans with a T-shirt and boots.

"I look like Maysun and Zandigay now!" Masha cried, feeling as strange in the village clothes as she had felt, not so long ago, in shorts and T-shirt.

"Yes, and you will be pretending to be their cousins, won't you? So it is good that you look like them. And who is Baba Musa?"

"Grandfather!" Kamala cried in Parvani.

Masha smiled shyly. "I like better to pretend you are our mother, Jana Khanum."

"Me, too," agreed Kamala solemnly.

Her heart hurt. "We'll pretend that again," she promised. "Are you all dressed? Good. Let's go back to Baba now. Maybe he has seen the markings on the helicopters."

Omar was in front of the house with the two Uzis and the entire supply of bullets. He looked up as the three arrived and nodded his approval.

"Khayli khoub," he said to the princesses.

He swung the strap over his shoulder with the barrel pointing to the ground and put several packs of ammunition into his pockets.

"Are you going to kill Jalal the bandit, Baba?" asked Masha.

"I will try, Masha," he said. He squinted up at the sky, but the helicopters were coming out of the sun and it was impossible to read the markings.

"They must start now," Omar told Jana in an aside. "If we wait till we see the markings, those in the helicopters will see the girls running."

"You know the way now," Jana told them. "I will take you a little way. Just stay on the path. Baba Musa will have heard the helicopters, and he will meet you on the path."

Omar said softly, *"Janam,* I ask you to go with them."

He had urged this before, when they made their plans, but she knew that to go with the girls to the village would mean certain discovery. She could not possibly pass as a villager, and it would be wrong to ask the villagers to risk their lives to hide her. "That they should risk their lives for the scion of the ruling family is a reasonable sacrifice to ask, Omar," she had said. "But not for me." Besides, she, too, had a tradition to live up to, as Omar himself had often pointed out. And it would kill her to run away and leave Omar to his fate, though this was an argument she did not put forward. She would rather be dead herself than hear of his death.

Now, that argument already won, she merely said, "No."

"Oh, Baba!" Masha cried. "Please cannot we stay and help you to kill Jalal the bandit? I would rather do that than leave you and Jana Khanum."

"Yes!" cried Kamala. "We will fight, Baba! We will be very brave!"

He knelt on the ground in front of them and wrapped his arms around his daughters, and felt how he now loved them in his heart. He had learned to love, perhaps too late.

"I am very proud that you are such brave princesses. When the time comes for you to rule this country, I know that you will do it well and be strong, Masha. And you will have Kamala to help you. I will always remember that to-day, you offered to stay and fight. Always. But it is more important for you to run now, so that one day you will rule. Will you do that for me?"

"Oh, Baba! I do not want to rule! I want to stay here with you and Jana Khanum and be happy!"

"I know. But a princess must sometimes do what is right for others even though she does not like the task."

Masha stifled her tears, and Jana led them off. She went a short way with them, down to the main path, then hugged them both very hard. There were tears in her eyes, but not in the eyes of Masha and Kamala. Their eyes were fixed on duty. The two princesses went stoically down the path towards the distant village, and Jana turned and blindly made her way back to Omar's side.

Jana and Omar stared after the princesses for a moment, but the sound of the helicopters was too insistent. She picked up the other Uzi and swung it over her shoulder as he had taught her, then reached for ammunition. They turned and squinted up into the sun again, but still they were only sinister black shadows.

"Four," said Omar. "Two of them Sikorskys. I have no Sikorskys. I don't think it can be Ashraf."

"Oh," was all Jana could say.

"Of course, only one can land here. There is no knowing what they mean to do with the others. It would be insane to bring the choppers in one at a time and land the troops—we could pick them off one by one. But I see no parachutists yet. We will know soon who they are."

They had planned for this moment. There was little they could do except take cover and aim well. But they had not imagined four helicopters. If it was Jalal they faced almost certain death or capture.

"Jana, this is not the time, but there may be no other. I am sorry to be so late saying it. I love you."

She caught her breath on a sob. "I love you, Omar."

"I have been a fool not to know my own heart before this. I know that I have loved you for a long time. From the beginning, probably. I remember that in my delirium I knew. Do you remember? Then I called you Beloved."

"I remember." She smiled at him. "So long ago."

"So long ago," Omar agreed. "And only last night did I understand myself. I would have come to wake you in a few minutes, to tell you. Then I heard them coming. So now—if this is Ashraf Durran, *Janam,* I ask you to marry me. Will you?"

Her heart was thumping hard enough to kill her. Tears burned her eyes. There was nothing she wanted more than this man beside her all the rest of her life, however long or short. But—

"And if it is Jalal?" she asked quietly.

"Then...who knows what will come?"

"You're asking me to marry you only on condition?"

He felt anger spurt in him. "On condition that I have something to offer you!"

"No. I will not marry you on conditions."

His anger left him as quickly as it had come. He put his free arm out to her. "*Janam,* do not give me such an answer," he pleaded. "Remember that you are my soul! You have said that you love me. How can I be divided from you?" He bent and tilted her chin, and gazed into her beautiful, shining eyes. "*Janam,*" he pleaded.

"I won't marry you on condition. If you want me, you want me come what may, the way I want you."

Every time he thought he had understood himself, or her, some new understanding came to show him how shallow his previous conception had been. Omar closed his eyes. What a woman she was! "This ancestor of yours—this king—what was his name?"

"Bonnie Prince Charlie," she said.

"Truly, he must have been a brave warrior, *Janam!* What a heart you have, my heart, my beloved!" He was not sure whether his own heart was breaking or only breaking its way out of a shell that had imprisoned it. He wanted to weep and to laugh at once. "You will marry me, then!"

"If you say to me now, we are married whatever comes, then I will marry you," she insisted.

With one hand he held his gun out of the way, with the other he swept her up against his chest and ruthlessly, hungrily, kissed her. "We are married, then, *Janam,* from this moment. You are mine!" He kissed her again, and her heart soared within her. "Say it!" he said, when he lifted his mouth again.

"I'm yours," she said, smiling mistily, as the sound of their fate came ever closer. "And you are mine."

His heart burst through the last of the bands that had imprisoned it, and he understood that he was happy. "My heart, my soul," he said, holding her tightly for another moment and then releasing her.

Then he looked up. One helicopter was closer than the others, and at last its markings were visible against the sun. Omar laughed and lifted one arm in a welcoming wave. "My brothers!" he said. "This helicopter is Rafi's! They have come to our rescue, Jana!"

Jana went down the path to the village to bring the princesses back, while Omar waited for the helicopter to land on the small space near the house that was the only suitable landing pad.

Karim did not wait for it to land. He jumped out while it was still several feet off the ground and ran towards his brother, clutching his gun to his side, his battle fatigues whipping in the wind that the great propellor stirred up.

"What the hell, Karim? You off to fight a war?" Omar demanded.

"Omar! Thank God you're alive!" Karim grabbed him in a bear hug and pounded his back while Omar returned the favour. "Is everything okay here?" Karim shouted in his ear. "*Ya Allah,* it's good to see you!"

"Everything is fine. What are you doing here?" he shouted, as Karim turned to the pilot and gave the thumbs-up signal. Inside the cockpit, Omar saw the pilot pick up his radio mike and talk, and overhead the other three helicopters changed direction.

Silence fell as the pilot on the ground killed his engines, and Omar saw that he was Rafi. After another minute Rafi jumped out and grabbed Omar in his turn, in a ruthless bear hug. "Good to see you!" he said, after a moment.

He was in battle fatigues, too. "What brings you here?" Omar asked again. He was feeling lightheaded. He had not seen either brother for two years, but somehow all that seemed to disappear. They were what they had always been to each other—the closest of brothers.

"What brings us here? I like that!" said Rafi. "Your damned messenger, that's what brings us here!"

"My—!" Omar said blankly. "What messenger? Come into the house and you can explain yourselves."

His brothers flung themselves down around the kitchen table while Omar made coffee. They explained, filling him in on all the details, including Aban Bahrami's patient wait outside Rafi's palace.

"He said you'd been shot down by Jalal. That right?" demanded Rafi.

"Fair's fair. I killed his horse," Omar said with a grin.

Rafi swore. "It's time we dealt with that son—" he said.

There was a momentary silence as the troubled subject seemed to bring up memories in all of them. Then Karim took the bull by the horns. "You were right, we should have dealt with him, Omar."

"We'll do it now," added Rafi.

Omar looked from one to the other and much that could not be said in words was said then. "Right," he agreed.

They discussed ways and means for a few moments, until the coffee was ready. Omar put cups on the table.

Rafi asked, "Where are Masha and Kamala? Not in bed?"

Omar shook his head. "We sent them down to the village. I didn't know if you were friend or foe."

"So that's why the welcoming party was armed! *Allah,* are you telling me Jalal has choppers now?"

"Not so far as I know. But it's always possible, isn't it?"

They nodded soberly. There might be half a dozen different sources willing to arm a man like Jalal, for any number of reasons. "We were damn stupid, letting it go for so long," Karim said again. "Anything could have happened."

"What exactly did happen, Omar?" Karim asked. "You sent off two flares, according to Aban, and then sent the message by Aban the next day saying you were in very deep and needed rescue.''

"One of the flares misfired when Jana tried to send it off. And I had no more.''

"Jana," Karim said slowly. "Is that the name of the English tutor who started it all? Ashraf says she took off with the kids. Is she crazy? How have you managed with her here all this time?''

"Pretty well," said Omar, with a slow smile.

At that moment there were running footsteps on the steps and then across the verandah, and the two princesses dashed into the kitchen, shouting, "Baba! Baba! Baba!" with wild, happy relief.

They flung themselves against him. "Baba, it was not Jalal the bandit! It was not Jalal the bandit!''

"No, it was not Jalal the bandit, children. Look who it was," he said. And while the princesses renewed their acquaintance with their two handsome uncles, Omar's eyes met Jana's across the room.

He put out his hand. "Come," he said.

She crossed the room to his side. He wrapped one arm around her and they stood smiling into each other's eyes while Masha and Kamala were thoroughly hugged.

"Meet my brothers, Jana," he said. "Karim, Rafi, this is Jana Stewart. She is going to be my wife.''

Seventeen

They arrived at the palace at nightfall, and climbed wearily out of the helicopter into the desert air. Umm Hamzah was waiting, wreathed in smiles. She hugged the princesses amid a babble of excited Arabic, and led them off to their beds.

Omar led Jana to her own bedroom, and kissed her lightly. "Will you join me later?" he asked.

She was exhausted, but also filled with happiness too rich to waste on sleep. "I'll feel fine after a bath," she assured him.

She relaxed in a scented tub, and washed her hair, revelling in the ease of it all. Just turn the tap and hot water gushes out! What a marvel! a part of her felt. And no need to ration shampoo! And the scent of perfumes! And such luxuriously fluffy towels, and so perfectly white and clean!

She dressed in the beautiful green outfit she had worn that first night that she and Omar had dined together, and put on makeup and jewellery for the first time in an age, and perfumed herself liberally. Then she went up to the terrace where, so long ago it seemed a different lifetime, they had eaten their meals together.

Omar was not, this time, in a Western suit. He was wearing a long, high-necked silk brocade jacket over baggy cream trousers, and brocade slippers, and looked every inch an Oriental monarch.

"Your Highness," she murmured.

And that was not the only way in which he had changed. His eyes and the set of his mouth were now very different from that first meeting, Jana realized, as Omar's full, generous lips moved into laughter. With one arm around her waist he caught her to him and kissed her.

"How many times you called me that!" he said. "Sometimes I wanted to shout at you—"

"Really? What did you want to say?"

Omar looked deep into her eyes. "I did not know," he said. "I know now, but then I only knew that you did it to annoy me and that it did annoy me."

Jana smiled. "Did it?"

"And yet there was no reason for it to do so."

A servant appeared with a bottle of champagne in a bucket of ice. "Mmm! Is this to celebrate our homecoming?" Jana asked.

"That, perhaps. Other things, too." The cork popped and the waiter filled two glasses and offered them on a silver tray. When they had taken the glasses, he bowed and discreetly disappeared.

They touched glasses and drank, then turned to stand side by side looking out over the desert. The moon was a tiny crescent hanging in the perfect navy sky, yet the desert seemed to glow as if it were mysteriously lighted from somewhere.

"It is so haunting," Jana murmured. "I'm sorry you don't like the desert. I find it fascinating."

"I no longer hate the desert," Omar said.

She turned in surprise. "No?"

"Loving you, there is much now that I love that I once did not."

She was filled with longing—to hold him, to crush him against her, to love him—there were no words to describe her need, the mysterious desire for perfect union that is impossible in this world.

"I love you, Omar," she whispered, in an aching voice, because just to tell it was a kind of release.

"I love you, Jana," he replied, and he bent down and his lips touched hers with gentle, loving passion. He set down his glass and turned to pick up a small velvet box.

"I want you to wear this," he said, and placed it on her palm.

She opened the box and took a long, slow breath. "Oh, Omar!"

The ring was made of a large, square-cut central sapphire on a square bed of rubies and diamonds. It was like nothing she had ever seen before, exotic and with a wild magic, in some ways like the cup.

"It belonged to my ancestress, the granddaughter of the great Queen Halimah," Omar told her. "She was said to be blessed with a happy life. Will you wear it for me?"

"It's utterly beautiful! Oh, yes, how can you ask? Is it my engagement ring?"

The look in his eyes was melting her as he lifted the ring out of the box and lifted her hand. The ring slipped over her finger and came to rest as if made for her.

"You did not ask it of me, you made other demands, my soul, but I swear to you that I will take no other wife but you," he said. Then he kissed her, and her heart leapt to her lips under the touch of his.

A few minutes later, when the servant entered to announce that dinner was ready, Omar led his fiancée to the table.

"Oh, how lovely to eat a meal that I haven't cooked and caught myself!" Jana exclaimed.

He smiled at her. "In truth, you are a companion both in trouble and in joy."

She smiled back. "You didn't think so that first night we ate here."

With a lazy look in his eye, he nodded his head. "Yes," he contradicted her. "If I was unbending with you then, it was because it was already necessary to control my reaction to you. It was too strong."

She heaved a sigh. So she had not been alone in feeling the attraction even then. "I certainly wished you weren't so controlled."

His eyes went dark. "Did you want me then?"

Jana only smiled. Omar laughed triumphantly, with a promising tone in the laughter that made her stomach shiver with anticipation.

Silence fell, and then he added, "My brother Karim tells me he, too, has found the woman he is going to marry. She is an American."

Jana smiled in delighted surprise. "That's perfect, isn't it? That will be so comfortable."

"He suggests that we have a joint state wedding."

Jana blinked. "State wedding!" she exclaimed. Suddenly it dawned on her that she was marrying a prince, the monarch of a country. Over the time at the lake, she had somehow managed to forget the impact of that fact. "Well, yes, I suppose it would be—" she lifted her shoulders "—just great, really."

Omar nodded.

"What a pity Rafi hasn't gotten himself engaged, too! Maybe we should wait until he finds someone?"

Omar smiled a smile that made her heart almost leap out of her breast. "No, we will not wait for that, *Janam*. It is enough that we have to have a state wedding, which will take much time. I can do this because I know my people would wish it very much. But I will not wait for Rafi. Rafi must look after himself. Jalal, too, can wait. I want to make you my wife as soon as it may be done,'' said Prince Omar.

* * * * *

Look for Prince Rafi's story,
BELOVED SHEIKH,
the third book in Alexandra Sellers's
romantic miniseries
SONS OF THE DESERT,
available in June 1999,
only from Silhouette Desire.

If you enjoyed what you just read,
then we've got an offer you can't resist!

Take 2 bestselling love stories FREE!

Plus get a FREE surprise gift!

‒‒‒‒‒‒‒‒‒‒

Clip this page and mail it to Silhouette Reader Service™

IN U.S.A.
3010 Walden Ave.
P.O. Box 1867
Buffalo, N.Y. 14240-1867

IN CANADA
P.O. Box 609
Fort Erie, Ontario
L2A 5X3

YES! Please send me 2 free Silhouette Desire® novels and my free surprise gift. Then send me 6 brand-new novels every month, which I will receive months before they're available in stores. In the U.S.A., bill me at the bargain price of $3.12 plus 25¢ delivery per book and applicable sales tax, if any*. In Canada, bill me at the bargain price of $3.49 plus 25¢ delivery per book and applicable taxes**. That's the complete price and a savings of over 10% off the cover prices—what a great deal! I understand that accepting the 2 free books and gift places me under no obligation ever to buy any books. I can always return a shipment and cancel at any time. Even if I never buy another book from Silhouette, the 2 free books and gift are mine to keep forever. So why not take us up on our invitation. You'll be glad you did!

225 SEN CNFA
326 SEN CNFC

Name	(PLEASE PRINT)	
Address	Apt.#	
City	State/Prov.	Zip/Postal Code

* Terms and prices subject to change without notice. Sales tax applicable in N.Y.
** Canadian residents will be charged applicable provincial taxes and GST.
   All orders subject to approval. Offer limited to one per household.
   ® are registered trademarks of Harlequin Enterprises Limited.

DES99   ©1998 Harlequin Enterprises Limited

SILHOUETTE® Desire®

May '99
LOVE ME TRUE
#1213 by ANN MAJOR

June '99
THE STARDUST COWBOY
#1219 by Anne McAllister

July '99
PRINCE CHARMING'S CHILD
#1225 by Jennifer Greene

August '99
THAT BOSS OF MINE
#1231 by Elizabeth Bevarly

September '99
LEAN, MEAN & LONESOME
#1237 by Annette Broadrick

October '99
FOREVER FLINT
#1243 by Barbara Boswell

MAN of the Month

MAN OF THE MONTH

For ten years Silhouette Desire
has been giving readers the ultimate in sexy,
irresistible heroes. Come join the celebration as some
of your favorite authors help celebrate our
anniversary with the most sensual, emotional love
stories ever!

Available at your favorite retail outlet.

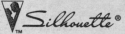

Silhouette®

FORTUNE'S Children™

**The Fortune family requests
the honor of your presence at the weddings of**

Silhouette Desire's scintillating new miniseries,
featuring the beloved Fortune family
and five of your favorite authors.

The Secretary and the Millionaire
by Leanne Banks (SD #1208, 4/99)

When handsome Jack Fortune asked his dependable assistant to
become his daughter's temporary, live-in nanny, Amanda Corbain
knew almost all her secret wishes had come true. But Amanda
had one final wish before this Cinderella assignment ended....

The Groom's Revenge
by Susan Crosby (SD #1214, 5/99)

Powerful tycoon Gray McGuire was bent on destroying the
Fortune family. Until he met sweet Mollie Shaw. And this sprightly
redhead was about to show him that the best revenge is...
falling in love!

Undercover Groom
by Merline Lovelace (SD #1220, 6/99)

Who was Mason Chandler? Chloe Fortune thought she knew
everything about her groom. But as their wedding day
approached, would his secret past destroy their love?

Available at your favorite retail outlet.

Look us up on-line at: http://www.romance.net   SDFORTUNE2

COMING NEXT MONTH

#1219 THE STARDUST COWBOY—Anne McAllister
Man of the Month/Code of the West
Seductive cowboy Riley Stratton claimed he had given up on happily-ever-after, but that didn't stop Dori Malone. When she and her son inherited half of the Stratton ranch, she was determined to show Riley that all of his forgotten dreams could come true...but only with her!

#1220 UNDERCOVER GROOM—Merline Lovelace
Fortune's Children: The Brides
Falling in love with her pretend fiancé was not part of Chloe Fortune's plan. But when she found out that he had a secret life, she fled. Now Mason Chandler was out to catch his runaway bride—and convince her that the only place to run was straight into his arms.

#1221 BELOVED SHEIKH—Alexandra Sellers
Sons of the Desert
One moment Zara was about to be kissed by handsome Sheikh Rafi, in the next she was kidnapped! And her captor was a dead ringer for the prince. Whom could she trust? Then "Rafi" appeared with a plan of rescue and a promise to make her queen. Was this a trap...or the only way back into the arms of her beloved sheikh?

#1222 ONE SMALL SECRET—Meagan McKinney
After nine years, Mark Griffin was back in town and playing havoc with Honor Shaw's emotions. Honor had never forgotten the summer she had spent in Mark's arms—and he wanted to pick up where they had left off. But would he still desire her once he learned her secret?

#1223 TAMING TALL, DARK BRANDON—Joan Elliott Pickart
The Bachelor Bet
Confirmed bachelor Brandon Hamilton had long ago given up on the idea of home, hearth and babies. But when he met stubborn beauty Andrea Cunningham, he found himself in danger of being thoroughly and irrevocably tamed....

#1224 THE WILLFUL WIFE—Suzanne Simms
Mathis Hazard didn't want anything to do with Desiree Stratford, but he couldn't turn his back on her need for protection. He agreed to help her as long as she followed *his* rules. But watching over Desiree each day—and night—had Mathis wondering if he was the one in danger...of losing his heart.